Nature of the Beast

Holly Copella

ISBN:
ISBN-13: 978-1-947694-37-8

To my dear friend,
Beverly Serfass

ACKNOWLEDGMENTS

Copella Books: First Paperback Edition 2026
Artwork By: Denise A. Werner
Cover Artist: Daniela Owergoor
Dani-owergoor.deviantart.com
Printed by CreateSpace, An Amazon.com Company

PUBLISHER'S NOTE

Chapter 1

The sea was mostly calm and still on the clear, bright night. The nine-million-dollar, ninety-five-foot Nordhaven yacht barely creaked while anchored in the middle of 'no man's land'. The "Sea Witch" had three decks and touted an impressive five bedrooms. One bedroom was on the second deck with access to the bridge and had its own balcony, while the other four bedrooms were below deck. With an open-concept floor plan, the first deck featured a decent-sized kitchen, dining room, and a living area that comfortably seated nine. There was a partially covered party deck at the ship's stern just off the living room. The top level was basically a party deck and even had a hot tub. It was just before dusk, and a thick fog seemed to roll steadily toward the yacht. The floating mansion gently rocked and creaked as the water suddenly rippled near it. A strange, massive swell passed the large vessel, causing it to rock.

The master bedroom on deck two belonged to the owner and captain of the "Sea Witch". The impressive bedroom was possibly larger than most city apartments and had twice as many amenities. To the right of the bed was the bridge entrance, and to the left was a full bathroom. There were two large windows, both aft and port side, although the blinds were drawn, and the double glass doors led to the private balcony at the stern. There was a small closet, two dressers, a large screen television, a built-in desk, a small refrigerator, and nightstands on either side of the bed. In addition to several scone wall lights, there were emergency lights beneath and above the bed. Cullen Holloway relaxed on top of the king-sized bed, which was still made. He hadn't yet changed for bedtime but was dozing off while reading the book in his hands. Cullen was a relatively attractive man in his late forties to early fifties of average height and a lean build. His dark hair was kept relatively short, although moderately spikey.

The yacht tilted sharply, and the loud creaking sound was heard from every corner of the vessel. Cullen just about dropped his book and looked around the cabin. He jumped from his bed, slipped into his shoes, and hurried outside. Cullen appeared on deck as the ship tilted again. He caught the railing, maintaining his balance, and rushed toward the ship's stern. He manned the large spotlight and scanned the mostly dark water. The light reflected off the dark depths of the water as it rippled. Cullen's eyes narrowed as he stared at the unusual swell that was often associated with whales. He then heard a faint splash from the aft side of the ship. Cullen was alerted to the sound and turned the spotlight aft. His eyes widened with surprise as he lifted the light upward and stared at the large image rising up alongside the ship.

§

Early morning. Gently lapping waves splashed against a large rock before rushing to the sandy shore.

As the waves raced back out to sea, a piece of white, broken fiberglass settled on the beach with the words, "Sea Witch" scrolled across it.

§

One week later. Holloway Art Gallery, located in the heart of the business district, had five gallery rooms, each with eight hundred square feet of exhibition space. The renovated building of more than four thousand square feet, which was once an old warehouse, housed hundreds of lavishly hung paintings and photographs, as well as more than two dozen sculptures displayed on tall marble stands. There were at least two open-style benches in each gallery for a relaxed viewing atmosphere. Each exhibition space had fifteen-foot walls painted a warm, mid-tone sage green, with an additional ten feet of sloped walls leading up to the cathedral ceilings, which were lit by many skylights. Wide, ten-foot-tall archways took visitors to the next segment of the gallery as the lightly stained hardwood floors creaked softly with every step of the dozens of visitors.

A young woman wearing a simple, fitted, knee-length black dress walked across the gallery, politely nodding to several guests as she passed. Brandy Holloway was a beautiful young woman in her early twenties with long dark hair and dark eyes. She stood about five-foot-six with a slightly athletic build, ample cleavage, and that classic, girl-next-door appeal. Brandy wasn't nearly as innocent as she looked, often attributing her mildly aggressive personality to her father, who abandoned her and her mother around the time she was born. In all actuality, she was a carbon copy of her mother. A fleet of caterers, dressed fashionably in black pants and white tops, buzzed around the art gallery-sponsored gala. Brandy glanced at her watch before looking around, somewhat bewildered. Some of their guests were already present with the rest on the way, and her mother was conspicuously missing.

The gala was her mother's big moment as an artist and the gallery owner, and she was somehow absent. Brandy removed her cell phone, prepared to text her when she saw her mother hurry across the gallery. Nadia Holloway was an attractive, well-dressed woman in her early to mid-forties with shoulder-length dark auburn hair. She was approximately five-foot-six with a moderately athletic build and a proud stature. Nadia wore an elegant peach colored, sleeveless dress with matching high heels. Despite Nadia seeming flushed and out of sorts, Brandy didn't question it. She was late for her own party. Of course, she was going to be out of sorts.

"Cutting it kind of close, aren't you?" Brandy asked her mother while indicating her watch. "A lot of your guests are already here."

Nadia couldn't seem to pull herself together and was more nervous than she should have been.

"I'm sorry," Nadia gasped and visibly trembled. "I just, well, I had a phone call."

Brandy immediately paused and held her breath before offering a tiny, sympathetic smile.

"Was it Gilford?" Brandy asked, then shook her head. "You need to let it go, Mom. Any man who goes on a five-day business trip that mysteriously turns into almost three weeks and barely even calls isn't worth stressing over."

"Gilford and I have been together for over three years," Nadia reminded her. "He's a good man."

"His business isn't important enough that he couldn't return for your gala tonight," Brandy informed her. "Face it. This was his way of ending the relationship, and he just wasn't man enough to do it face-to-face." She hesitated. "I love Gilford, too, but you have to know when to let go."

"Thanks for making me feel worse," Nadia muttered, then shook her head. "But it wasn't Gilford who called."

"Oh?" Brandy asked with surprise. "Then who was it?"

"One of your father's closest friends," Nadia informed her almost timidly.

Brandy's expression immediately dropped into a sneer. "I don't have a father," she remarked, lacking emotion.

"Well, you're right about that," Nadia replied, appearing defeated. "His boat sank in the Caribbean Sea near Costa Rica sometime last week. He's presumed dead."

Brandy eyed her mother with some surprise at the news. After the initial shock wore off, her hostility quickly returned.

"Please tell me you're not upset about it," Brandy remarked. "He was a horrible husband to you. The man abandoned you right after I was born."

Nadia fidgeted and looked down, obviously saddened by the news, despite the truths her daughter was spouting.

"He *was* a good husband," Nadia replied delicately. "He was just fighting his own demons, and I'd forgiven him for abandoning us." She finally looked up and met Brandy's gaze. "I would think you'd forgive him as well, for my sake."

"Stop saying he was a good man," Brandy insisted, becoming almost animated. "Good men don't abandon their wives and babies."

"I know you don't understand," Nadia informed her. "Maybe, one day, you will. I loved that man with every ounce of my heart. Just because his demons took him away from me, that doesn't mean I'll ever stop loving him."

Brandy drew a deep breath and sighed while shaking her head. "I'm sorry, Mom," she remarked.

"He doesn't deserve your sorrow or any other emotions." She then indicated the galleries. "You're missing your big moment. You'd better fix your makeup and pull yourself together."

Chapter 2

Two days later. Brandy walked on the well-groomed path along the outer edge of the park alongside another woman close to her own age. It was a beautiful, warm day with plenty of sunshine, and the park had more visitors than its fair share. Brandy's friend, Eva Jericho, was slightly taller than average, being almost five-foot-seven with a fairly athletic build. With straight dark hair and equally dark eyes, Eva was considered a natural beauty. She didn't wear any makeup, refused to wear dresses, and at times talked like a sailor on shore leave, yet she was pursued by plenty of men, despite never doing the chasing. Since she went for the 'bad boy' type, naturally, the men she was most attracted to weren't often the ones best suited for her. Since she was only in her early twenties, she had plenty of time to worry about a serious relationship later. For now, it was all artists, musicians, and gym rats.

"The gala was everything my mother could ever have hoped it would be," Brandy informed her friend while attempting to push all her bad feelings aside. "I think this was the push the gallery needed to become successful."

"Why are you evading my question?" Eva just about demanded.

Brandy avoided looking at her friend while showing little emotion. "I don't feel anything," she replied. "Does that make you happy? My father's dead, and I don't feel a damned thing."

"You must feel something," Eva insisted. "You wouldn't be human if you didn't have some sort of feelings about his death."

"Anger," Brandy finally blurted out, matter-of-factly. "Anger that he ran out on my mother right after I was born. Anger that he had the nerve to die without ever seeing his own daughter." She frowned and shook her head. "The man was a bastard, despite my mother's skewed opinion of him. I wouldn't doubt he was probably some perverted Playboy."

"Okay," Eva replied with a gentle sigh. "Anger is an appropriate emotion, given the situation." She then shifted, now uncomfortable. "Are you going to the funeral? Would you like some moral support?"

"There was a memorial service yesterday, but I couldn't force myself to go," Brandy informed her. "I can't feel remorse for the loss of some man I didn't even know. He may have been my biological father, but he meant nothing to me, and he was pure misery for my mother."

"How's she taking his death?" Eva asked, cringing at the potential response.

"I think she still had feelings for the bastard," Brandy remarked. "As if she didn't have enough problems with Gilford dumping her."

"Gilford dumped her?" Eva asked, somewhat surprised. "I thought they had a good relationship. I liked him. He was a lot of fun."

"Yeah, well," Brandy huffed. "I guess it doesn't pay to get attached. Gilford had been like a father to me these past few years. Then, he took off three weeks ago, barely called, and finally stopped calling altogether. I should have known he'd break her heart, too."

Eva shifted uncomfortably and seemed at a loss for words. "I feel bad for your mother," she remarked. "She can't seem to catch a break when it comes to love." Eva again shifted and grimaced slightly. "Maybe we should go out another time. Or just make it a girls' night out."

Brandy turned to face her friend and offered a warm smile. "No, you're allowed to be happy in a relationship, Eva. Just because I hate men right now, that doesn't mean you have to hide your boyfriend from me. Dexter seems like a nice guy, and I'd like to get to know him better."

"Feels like rubbing salt in a wound," Eva muttered, then shivered slightly. "But if you're finished mourning the loss of your father, you and Paula can meet us at the club tonight."

"Yes, I'm definitely finished mourning," Brandy replied with a soft chuckle, then immediately frowned. "Just not finished cursing."

They heard a falcon's caw as it flew overhead. Both looked up and watched the bird gracefully gliding on the warm, gentle breeze.

Chapter 3

The nightclub interior featured varying shades of purple, from the dark purple ceiling and walls to the light purple carpeting and U-shaped leather booths. The ceiling had a massive light that looked like a diamond, with strip lighting fanning out in every direction, while spotlights around the room changed color and rotated at random. In addition to nearly a dozen large booths that easily seated eight or more people, there were smaller tables and even some standing counter space. The massive bar, with several bartenders, was standing-room-only. The dance floor was big enough to accommodate one hundred people, though not comfortably. The place was packed, and it was loud with pulsating electronic dance music that seemed to play the same song on an endless loop. The nightclub was unusually crowded for a Thursday evening, as it was ladies' night. The mostly twenty-something crowd drank, danced, and socialized within the loud, smoke-filled room.

Brandy sat at a smaller table with another woman in her early twenties, Paula. Paula Dunn was an attractive young woman with shoulder-length, golden-brown hair and big brown eyes. She was a petite woman, standing about five-foot-four. Paula was the opposite of her friend, Eva. She loved dressing up, wearing makeup, and acting the part of a lady, even if she could trash-talk with the best of them. Brandy and Paula already had their drinks when Eva approached their table with a handsome man by her side. Dexter was everything Brandy and Paula had come to expect from one of Eva's boyfriends. He was almost six-foot-two, built moderately athletic to muscular, and about as handsome as a man could be. He had short dark hair that was moderately spikey on top, medium-length sideburns, and a mostly clean-shaven face. The man in his late twenties had a killer smile, which was undoubtedly hard for most women to resist, and he had a bold, outgoing personality with the ability to charm everyone.

Naturally, Eva's friends were a little jealous of her latest and greatest boyfriend. Being an artist should have sealed the deal, but all her artist boyfriends over the last few years weren't making any money off their work. With his job at the radio station, he managed to pay his own way. Dexter appeared very attentive to Eva once they sat down, placing his arm around her while sitting close.

"Ladies," Dexter announced proudly. "Next round is on me."

"Really?" Paula remarked while grinning. "What's the occasion?"

Eva smiled as she clung to her boyfriend. "Dexter got his first commission check."

"You sold one of your sculptures?" Brandy asked. "That's terrific!"

"My first one," Dexter announced proudly.

"I thought you worked for a radio station," Paula remarked.

"I work at the radio station to 'get by'," he informed Paula. "But I'm actually an artist. The real kind."

Dexter offered a tiny, tense smile. "You know, the starving kind."

"I didn't know you were an artist too," Paula announced, then indicated Brandy. "Brandy's mother owns a--"

Brandy nudged Paula, appearing uncomfortable. She didn't want her friend mentioning her mother's art gallery to a starving artist. It would only be a matter of time before the standard follow-up question was asked, and Brandy didn't have any influence over the art her mother displayed and sold in her gallery.

Paula took her cue and gently cleared her throat. "Brandy's mother is an artist too."

"Yes, I've heard," Dexter replied a little too cheerfully. "Eva said she owns that gallery in the business district."

It was foolish of Brandy to assume he didn't already know about that from Eva. Of course, Eva told him about the gallery. It would naturally come up in conversation. Rather a starving artist than the one guy Eva dated around the time she graduated high school. The professional gamer. Who even knew there was such a thing? At least Eva seemed happy, and Dexter was attentive enough. Perhaps a little too attentive. Brandy eyed the happy couple, sitting in a close huddle, talking in hushed tones, their lips almost touching. Yes, Brandy was a little envious of her friend. Eva was actually giddy, which was fun to watch, especially considering she wasn't even drunk yet. While Paula and Eva discussed Dexter's recent commission on his artwork and his work at the radio station, Brandy zoned out, getting lost in her own world. She snapped out of her thoughts when she realized Paula was staring at her.

"You're unusually quiet," Paula remarked, then appeared curious. "Something wrong?"

"I don't want to ruin anyone's good time tonight," Brandy insisted. "I'll tell you another time."

"No, tell us," Paula insisted. "Did something happen? Is it Gilford?" Her look turned sympathetic. "Did he dump your mother?"

"Well, that happened too," Brandy remarked before shifting uncomfortably. "I was contacted this afternoon by the lawyer representing my father's estate. He wants me to meet him tomorrow morning. Apparently, I've been mentioned in his will."

"Your father died?" Dexter asked, genuinely surprised. "Oh, I'm sorry to hear."

Eva lightly jabbed him in the side and gave him a commanding look.

"Oh," Dexter muttered, then grimaced while sinking into his seat. "I forgot."

"It's not a disease, people," Brandy informed them.

"Just didn't want to make you uncomfortable," Paula insisted.

"Please," Brandy moaned. "Your attempt at not making me uncomfortable is making me very uncomfortable."

"Enough of this talk," Eva announced, interrupting the conversation to spare her friend. "Let's get out there and dance."

"You guys go," Brandy remarked. "I'll wait for the waitress and order another round."

"Remember," Dexter announced as he stood with Eva. "That round is on me."

"I won't forget," Brandy replied.

While left alone at the table, Brandy remained preoccupied. She wished the entire business with her absentee father's death hadn't been living rent-free in her head, but she couldn't stop thinking about it. Maybe it had more to do with her mother's love for the guy who abandoned them. Brandy was still in her own world when the waitress approached their table with refills for all four, surprising Brandy, since she hadn't even ordered yet.

"The gentleman at the bar bought the next round," the cocktail waitress informed her, then indicated the bar.

Brandy glanced across the nightclub but didn't see the man in question. When she looked back at the waitress, the young woman seemed equally puzzled.

"I don't see him," the waitress remarked, then smiled and waved it off. "I'll point him out the next time I see him."

Although it wasn't uncommon for men to buy drinks for her and her friends, that didn't usually apply when another man was present at their table. Another man sort of defeated the purpose of buying the ladies drinks. Since the drinks were already delivered, Brandy decided she had better join her friends. As she made her way across the crowded dance floor without being stepped on, bumped, or knocked over, she finally found them. Paula and Eva were dancing to the fast song and having a good time, but Dexter was conspicuously missing. Brandy was about to tap Eva and question her boyfriend's disappearance when they heard a commotion and a scream, followed by a crash, from the bar area. Since there might be a fight in progress, everyone always looked. All three joined the rest of the crowd to have a look.

A table was overturned, and a man was pulling himself to his feet while touching the cut on the corner of his mouth. To their horror, the man scraping himself off the floor was Dexter! He straightened and looked around the bar, attempting to find the man who'd hit him. Brandy hurried across the club and approached, but there was no sign of the man who started the fight.

"Are you okay?" Brandy asked and again scanned the area. "What happened?"

"I'm fine," Dexter snarled in anger and embarrassment, then touched his bleeding lip. "Damned irritable people in this place."

Eva and Paula quickly joined them after noticing the aftermath.

"What happened?" Eva gasped, concerned as she briefly checked over her boyfriend. "Were you in a fight?"

"No, I wasn't in a fight," Dexter insisted while dusting himself off. "Some guy just took a swing at me. Unprovoked. Probably bumped into him and didn't even realize it."

"We'd better return to the table before he comes back," Paula informed her friends.

"You ladies wait at the table," Dexter announced, becoming increasingly agitated and moderately unpredictable. "I'll be right back."

As Dexter turned to leave, Eva stared at him with surprise. "Where are you going?" she asked.

"Nowhere," he scoffed. "I'm just going to see if the bastard is still here."

As Dexter turned and pushed through the crowd, Eva frowned and shook her head.

"I'll never understand men," Eva retorted. "They just go looking for fights."

"No, Eva," Paula announced with a sigh. "Just the ones you date." She then nodded across the nightclub. "Let's go back to the table. I need a drink."

§

When Dexter finally returned to their table twenty minutes later, his mood had changed entirely. It didn't matter whether he was sulking or fuming; it was killing Eva's good time. Unfortunately, Brandy and

Paula relied on Eva to keep the good times rolling when they went out.

"Can't you just let it go?" Eva finally demanded, after more than an hour of her boyfriend's brooding.

"It's personal, Eva," Dexter informed her somewhat bitterly.

"How can it be personal if the two of you hadn't even interacted?" Paula asked, questioning the truthfulness of his original story.

Dexter glared at Paula, projecting his irritability onto her. "He *did* attack me unprovoked," he insisted. "But the waitress also told me that the guy who sucker punched me was the same guy who bought a round of drinks for the table."

Brandy was now interested in what had actually happened. "Are you suggesting he was trying to force out the competition?" she asked.

"It crossed my mind," Dexter replied, then cast a quick look at Eva. "Which means he'd potentially taken an interest in you."

"That does change the dynamic a bit," Eva insisted, now suspicious.

"If Eva has an aggressive secret admirer, maybe we should call it a night and go home," Paula suggested. "The last thing you want to do is engage some creepy weirdo."

"Paula's right," Brandy replied. "I don't think any of us is having a good time anymore anyway."

Eva looked at Dexter and smiled affectionately while quite possibly placing her hand on his leg under the table.

"We can have our own party back at your place," Eva announced, then winked. "Just the two of us."

Dexter finally smiled and nodded. "I can't argue with that," he replied, then looked at Paula and Brandy. "Did you guys need a ride home?"

"No, we have my car," Brandy insisted. "We're good."

As Eva and Dexter got up to leave, Eva smiled at Brandy.

"I'll see you at the apartment tomorrow afternoon," Eva announced, then left with Dexter.

Paula watched them leave, then eyed Brandy. "One shot for the road?"

"I'm buying," Brandy announced with a light groan.

"Why is it Eva always gets the stalkers?" Paula lightly pouted. "Did you ever notice that?"

Brandy eyed her friend somewhat skeptically. "Are you actually jealous that you don't have a stalker?" she asked.

Paula offered a tiny smile and shrugged. "Maybe."

Both women laughed.

Chapter 4

Brandy slept somewhat restlessly that night, as she had the last two nights since learning about her father's death. She had horrifying nightmares about Cullen's boat sinking and feeling as if she, herself, were drowning. The dreams made no sense to her since she had no sympathy toward the man who abandoned her as a baby. In line with most city apartments, Brandy's shared residence with Eva was small. It had two bedrooms, a small living room, a tiny kitchen, and a shared bathroom. Anything bigger would cost too much. Despite both of them making decent money, rent was still ridiculously expensive, and there was little point wasting money on a bigger place when it was wiser to save money for their future instead. Brandy's small bedroom was just big enough to fit her double bed, a tall dresser, and a nightstand. Thankfully, there was a decent-sized closet, though she kept most of her personal belongings at her mother's house.

Even though she could have stayed living with her mother, Eva needed her own place but couldn't afford to live by herself. Moving in together seemed like a good idea at the time. Sometimes, her little apartment felt like freedom, but other times, it felt like a tiny prison cell. Since their apartment was in the basement, each room had only a small window, and the walls were cinder-block painted white. The cement floor was covered with hardwood, but it still got exceptionally cold in winter. After Gilford walked out on her mother a couple of weeks ago, Brandy started thinking about her much larger, brighter, and warmer bedroom back at her mother's house. Was it wrong to think about moving back home and possibly taking Eva with her? There was more than enough room. A thought for another day. It was a little after three o'clock in the morning, and only two hours since she'd gone to bed after their night out. Even though she lacked quality sleep, she still managed to have multiple vivid and even violent dreams.

As she just about drifted off after another nightmare, she felt a shadow loom over her. Brandy abruptly opened her eyes and just about shot up in bed, mildly panicked. Her bedroom curtains gently flapped inward from the warm night breeze through the small open window. Brandy stared at her bedroom window a moment, not recalling if she had actually opened it. She clutched the sheet against her body and shivered despite the moderately warm night. Her mind replayed chilling scenes from her most recent nightmares. While lost in her thoughts, she caught a glimpse of a shadow passing by her partially open bedroom door. It was then that Brandy realized there was a light on in the living room. She didn't remember opening her bedroom window, but she definitely remembered shutting off the living room and kitchen lights. Brandy climbed out of bed, wearing her sleep shorts and tank top, and cautiously left her bedroom. She wasn't sure what had her so on edge lately, but she'd been filled with a sense of dread and the feeling that she was being watched ever since the news of her father's death.

Brandy entered the living room in what could only be described as 'stealth mode'. The living room slash kitchen area was only a little bigger than Brandy's bedroom. The kitchen consisted of a sink, a stove with an oven, and a couple of cupboards. There was an island counter with a few more cupboards that also doubled as their eating area, comfortably seating three people. Their sofa was backed up against the island counter, giving a three-foot walkway between it and the opposing wall with their decent-sized television mounted on the cinderblock wall. The only nice thing about the basement apartment was its outside entrance. They didn't have to go through the main entrance, unless they wanted to. Brandy glanced around the well-lit apartment interior. Naturally, she didn't see anything, and why would she? She was being ridiculous and paranoid! Brandy then heard a faint creaking sound, and her eyes immediately shifted to the front door. It was partially open!

Brandy stared at the door for a moment, confused and concerned, before cautiously approaching it. She gently pushed the door shut, then flipped the dead bolt with an unusual urgency. She released the breath she'd been holding and finally felt her body relax. As she turned, a large black cat jumped onto the table alongside the door. Brandy cried out with surprise, startling the cat. She stared at the cat for a moment, trying to calm her pounding heart, then sighed with relief and smiled.

"Who are you?" Brandy asked the cat sweetly, then picked it up and held it to her chest. The cat immediately purred and rubbed its head beneath her chin. "You must belong to the new people across the hall." Brandy stroked the purring, affectionate cat. "Don't let the landlady see you. You'll be out on your tail."

Brandy loved animals but lived in a 'pet-free' apartment building. Not surprisingly, just about everyone in the building was secretly harboring a cat or a small dog. Since she only moved into the apartment a year ago, Brandy wasn't ready to invoke her landlady's wrath by harboring a forbidden pet. She didn't want to give the landlady another reason to complain. Brandy unlocked and opened the door, then nuzzled the cat once more before ushering it into the hallway.

"Come back and visit another time," she told the cat, then shut and locked the door behind it.

As Brandy turned, she nearly collided with Eva, who was suddenly standing behind her. Brandy jumped and screamed, prompting Eva to jump and scream as well. Both women held their pounding hearts as they silently stared at the other. Eva was still dressed from their evening at the club.

"Jesus, Brandy," Eva gasped. "Don't do that!"

"You scared the crap out of me," Brandy cried out while attempting to control her breathing. "You said you weren't coming home tonight."

Eva frowned and returned to the living room while toting a pint of ice cream. She flopped onto the sofa with a disgusted sigh.

"Dexter is such a bastard," Eva scoffed, then pouted. "He dumped me!"

Despite her surprise that the 'dumping' hadn't been the other way around, Brandy approached and sat on the edge of the sofa while offering a sympathetic look.

"What happened?" Brandy asked. "You guys seemed fine when you left the table."

"We were getting ready to leave when he suddenly took off," Eva remarked. "Apparently, he saw that guy again and chased him down. They got into it in the nearby alleyway. By the time I got there, the guy had already pummeled his ass and left. Dexter looked like hell." She frowned and ate a spoonful of ice cream. "Serves him right for going after that guy." She hesitated, then finally looked at Brandy. "We got into this big fight right there in the alley about it, and he told me he didn't want to see me anymore." Eva shifted uncomfortably while lost in thought. "I don't know. Maybe I was wrong and should apologize. Maybe I was a little harsh for berating him for chasing that guy into the alley."

"You weren't in the wrong," Brandy insisted, almost too quickly, then attempting to walk back her eagerness to berate Dexter. "You're better off without some guy who goes looking for a fight anyway."

"You're right," Eva replied with a defeated sigh while taking another large spoonful of ice cream. "I wish I didn't go for the 'bad boys'." She then hesitated. "Or the artist types." Her frown further increased. "Or musicians." She finally met Brandy's gaze. "I think it's the thrill of dating those kinds of guys." She then considered the comment and shrugged. "And the sex." Eva shook her head. "Maybe I should give up on men and seek thrills elsewhere. You know, like skydiving or something."

They exchanged looks, then immediately chuckled in unison.

Eva continued seeking comfort in her ice cream. "Anyway," she announced with a sigh. "I didn't mean to wake you."

Brandy collapsed onto the sofa near Eva and sighed with disgust. "I wasn't sleeping very well anyway," she replied.

Eva eyed her friend sympathetically. "Are you still thinking about your father?"

"I'd be lying if I said I haven't thought twice about him," Brandy replied. "But my never-ending parade of gruesome nightmares says otherwise." She then looked at her friend with some uncertainty. "I was planning on canceling my appointment with my father's lawyer, but now I'm not so sure. Do you think I should meet the guy and get it over with?"

"Definitely," Eva immediately chirped. "Maybe he left you something of some value. Make up for the pain he's caused you and your mother."

"I don't want anything from him," Brandy insisted.

Eva glared at Brandy and raised a commanding brow. Brandy held her breath a moment while staring at her friend.

"I suppose you're right," Brandy replied with a sigh. "I'll meet with the damned lawyer."

Brandy heaved herself off the sofa, said goodnight, and returned to her room, leaving the bedroom door open. The light from the living room provided just enough brightness to find her bed easily. Brandy pulled the covers back, then climbed in and suddenly hesitated. She saw four large tears along the fitted sheet on the left-hand side of the bed. Brandy eyed the torn, fitted sheet and ran her fingers over the tears. She hesitated a moment, then looked around the dimly lit room.

Chapter 5

Late morning. Stone walls and a large, open iron gate surrounded the well-kept country estate of more than twenty acres. Brandy drove down the long driveway lined with weeping willows while periodically checking her car's dashboard GPS. She was convinced she was lost, almost sure she wasn't supposed to be on this particular private lane. The impressive driveway, although elegant, seemed to stretch on without end. She finally reached a large clearing and saw the enormous, possibly haunted, mansion before her. The mansion was dark gray stone, pure Scottish Baronial, two and a half menacing stories of architectural beauty, and looking much like a 16th-century fortified castle. A steeply pitched slate roof, bristling with chimneys, seemingly rose up from the depths of hell. Tapering turrets, crow-stepped gables, and pepper-pot bartizans reached up to the storm-wracked skies.

Flanking the deep entrance, two semi-circular drum towers lunged forward. Their third-story dormers were crowned by elaborate scrolled pediments and tiny iron-railed balconies that seemed designed for watching rather than admiring. The long driveway went straight back to the detached garage and also wrapped around a large, three-level marble water fountain in front. Brandy pulled up alongside the fountain and a fancy red Porsche, obviously belonging to the attorney. The lawyer stood outside his car, smiling as she got out. Attorney Rockwell was possibly in his early to mid-thirties. He was a surprisingly handsome man with a tall, lean frame. His dark hair was kept short yet stylish, but the growth of stubble on his face seemed out of place. His wardrobe also needed a little help. His suit wasn't of the highest quality and seemed ill-fitted. If Brandy hadn't known any better, she would have suspected he was either an undercover cop or a bum. Either way, his credentials checked out.

Rockwell approached her with a broad grin and extended his hand. "Ms. Holloway," he announced cheerfully. "Thank you for taking the time to meet me all the way out here."

Brandy shook his hand and immediately felt something was off about her father's attorney. Her instincts about people were usually pretty good. Something about the vibe he projected put her a little on edge. Perhaps it was the combination of a cheap suit and an expensive car that unsettled her. Oddly enough, the strange energy seemed to come directly from the handshake itself. Brandy was quick to pull her hand back and immediately shifted while attempting to hide her discomfort. She refocused her attention by glancing at the impressive yet extremely creepy-looking mansion.

"This is some place you have," she remarked, attempting to shift her focus, then chuckled. "You must be one hell of a lawyer and a fan of horror movies."

Brandy immediately cursed herself for pointing out the house's bizarre nature to the man who had aroused her distrust.

Rockwell cocked his head, possibly confused, then smiled and chuckled. "Well, I am, thank you," he replied, then indicated the house while holding up the house keys. "But this was your father's estate." He then extended the keys to her. "The estate in all its entirety was left to you, per his will."

Brandy eyed him almost suspiciously while accepting the keys. "You're kidding, right?"

"I wouldn't kid about real estate," Attorney Rockwell announced, seeming quite pleased. "Your father left everything to you." He then indicated the mansion before them. "The house is quite amazing. The kitchen, two dining rooms, formal living room, family room, game room, two-story library, two-story study, ballroom, sunroom, and four powder rooms are all located on the first floor. Off the kitchen, there are also four staff bedrooms with two shared baths. On the second floor, there are ten bedrooms, each with its own full bath, and a laundry room. The smaller third floor has an artist's workshop, a conservatory, a second sunroom, a child's playroom, and a full bathroom."

Just when Brandy thought the attorney had finished making her head spin with all the rooms, he continued.

"In the finished basement, there's a wine cellar with a cigar lounge, and a home theater with a shared powder room," Rockwell informed her. "Adjacent to that, there's a gym, including a steam room, and a full bath. There's also an unfinished basement with its own entrance, but it's a little creepy down there."

A little creepy? Was he kidding? There was something in the mansion that was creepier than the exterior? Brandy barely made sense of his words while he continued rambling off the many amenities the mansion offered.

"Out back, there's a large garden, a pool with an attached hot tub, a patio containing a party kitchen, and a pool house with a full bath," the lawyer announced. "The estate is over forty acres and has a detached, eight-car garage with living quarters above it and a gardener's workshop next to that." Rockwell seemed proud while looking over the structure. "The mansion is an exquisite work of art. It has natural stone, original hand-carved woodwork, and eight handcrafted fireplaces. There are also four staircases, not including the two basement ones. The grand staircase, the one in the study, the one in the library, and one in the kitchen."

Brandy shifted several looks from the mansion, which appeared to have all the comfort of the "Psycho" house and all the charm of "The Addams Family" home, to Rockwell.

"I'm afraid I don't understand," she announced. "I was under the impression my father was a bum as well as an asshole. My mother never mentioned that he was a rich asshole."

Rockwell appeared slightly surprised by the comment but quickly resumed his smile. "No, I assure you, he was quite wealthy," he informed her. "Not too many bums own nine million dollar yachts."

"Was that his boating accident?" Brandy asked, now curious for the first time. "A nine-million-dollar yacht?"

"Unfortunately, yes," Rockwell replied before guiding her to the steps.

Five broad steps, guarded by a pair of four-foot stone dragons coiled atop squat pillars, wings half-spread, mouths open in a permanent warning, led up to a carved stone archway. The main entrance had tall, double doors, possibly carved out of centuries-old wood and lavishly hand-detailed. Adorned with wrought iron, the entranceway was perhaps the gates to hell itself. Despite being moderately intimidated by the gothic-style mansion, Brandy couldn't seem to take her focus off what she felt was more important at the moment.

"So my father abandoned my mother and me without a dime, but he was worth millions?" Brandy scoffed, becoming irritated all over again as she followed the lawyer up the massive steps, taking a moment to eye the stone dragons.

Rockwell paused before the large front doors and eyed Brandy with some surprise. "I don't think that's entirely accurate," he informed her. "Although I'm not aware of the reasons surrounding his departure from you or your mother, he had given your mother that art gallery in the city, the house outside of town, and set up a trust fund for your continuing education."

Brandy stared at him, still confused. "My mother never told me that," she remarked somewhat softly. "I wonder why?"

Rockwell shrugged. "Perhaps she was a woman scorned," he replied. "Perhaps Cullen was an asshole. I couldn't really say. I just know the financial aspect of his life."

"No, she wasn't a woman scorned," Brandy assured him. "Quite the opposite. She always spoke fondly of him."

"I wish I knew," Rockwell remarked while opening the door. "He left his journal as part of your inheritance. Perhaps there's something in there to help fill in the blanks."

Rockwell extended his hand at the open doorway, allowing her to enter first. Brandy eyed the opening, somewhat apprehensively, but reluctantly entered.

Chapter 6

Passing through the main entrance into the massive foyer, Brandy stopped and looked around in stunned silence. The grand hallway was at least sixteen feet wide and appeared to extend forever, traveling past many rooms situated on either side. A set of immense double doors at the end of the corridor remained shut. Brandy was rather curious as to what was behind them. Several massive, long tapestry carpets, mostly covering the old slate floor, were in a bold mauve-and-gold print. The fifteen-foot-tall walls were rounded stone with tall stone archways above each set of large wooden doors. There were antique tables and chairs along the walls, as well as huge, strange, old paintings in colossal frames. The tall, exposed beam ceiling had many non-frilly chandeliers to light the never-ending corridor, while wall-mounted lights resembling candles were posted on either side of every doorway.

The many lights would brighten the otherwise dark hallway, with the only other light coming through the wall of windows on the staircase landing. In addition to the antique furnishings within the broad, massive hallway, there were old, fully intact suits of armor posted on both sides of the eight doorways. Possibly installed on mannequins, they appeared real enough, standing tall and rigid, each with their broadsword, shield, or spear in hand. The sheer size and apparent wealth were enough to overwhelm her, but she was more taken aback by the abundance of creepiness. Naturally, her eyes fell upon the crowning glory of the first floor. The grand staircase was a hand-carved masterpiece in rich mahogany. The railing pillars on either side of the stairs held matching dragon lamps with large, spread wings. Rising from each of the dragon's backs was the lamp post and crimson red glass shades with sculpted metal on both the top and bottom of the glass. While lit, they gave a creepy reddish glow to the staircase.

The broad steps, with a bold mauve carpet down the center similar to that in the grand hallway, led up to a small landing boasting a large stained-glass window depicting two jousting knights with a castle in the background. One medieval knight in silver armor rode a white horse while the second wore black armor and rode a black horse. The staircase branched off both left and right to the second floor. Each staircase also led up to the third floor. The rungs beneath the banisters were hand-carved in intricate detail. Rockwell immediately guided Brandy to the study a few doors down the grand hallway. She barely kept up, wanting to linger and peer into each room, partly out of awe and partly out of sheer fright. She hoped he'd give her the grand tour after he finished with the formalities, because she certainly didn't want to explore the house on her own.

Rockwell opened the study door and again allowed her to enter first. The massive, two-story study seemed to keep in theme with the whole gothic vibe the mansion had going. Looking more like a smaller library, there was a decorative, dark-wood, winding staircase leading to the second floor, which had even more bookcases than the first. The hardwood floor was covered with a massive, mauve, cranberry, and black throw rug. A large, detailed mahogany fireplace was opposite the main bookcase and a large leather chair. The huge, antique desk was toward the back of the study, beyond the curved stairs. Another bookcase was behind the desk between two, floor-to-ceiling windows. Brandy couldn't believe what she was seeing. Even the study was a frightening work of art! The creep vibes were off the chart, yet she couldn't stop admiring the room even while following Rockwell toward the antique desk. He set his briefcase on the marble top and began opening several drawers on the desk. It was the lawyer's turn to appear confused. He opened every drawer, growing more concerned.

"I could've sworn--" Rockwell muttered while again rummaging through the first drawer, now distracted. "Your father's black, leather-bound journal was supposed to be locked in his desk drawer." He briefly looked up while continuing his search. "He was very specific that I hand it to you personally."

"Could he have taken it with him on his yacht?" Brandy asked.

Rockwell hesitated, shut the last drawer, and finally met her gaze. "It's possible," he replied. "Maybe it's in his bedroom or the library."

"I'm sure it'll turn up," Brandy replied, lacking interest in her 'so-called' father's personal thoughts. His private journal was of no interest to her.

"Yes, I hope it does," Rockwell announced, showing more concern than she had. "There was concern that his son may have wanted the journal, but it was his wish that you maintain possession of it."

Despite barely paying attention, Brandy caught on to what he'd said. "He had a son? I have a half-brother?" she gasped, somewhat stunned. Her look turned harsh, and she snorted a laugh. "I wonder if he was a better father to him."

"I don't really know much about your half-brother, Ford," Rockwell informed her. "And I wasn't left any instructions regarding contacting him either."

"I can't believe I have a half-brother," she remarked, lost in thought for only a moment. "Maybe I was better off having an absentee father than the one Ford knew."

"I'm sure you have a lot of questions about your father," Rockwell announced, then removed a phonebook from the desk drawer and paged through it.

"I have more questions about this house than my father," Brandy muttered, not loud enough for him to hear.

"A friend of your father's called my office shortly after his death was announced." He found the page he was looking for. "Ah, here it is. His name is Xaroc Nevar. Sounds Russian, I think." He casually shrugged. "I'm not sure how much help he'd be, but you could try calling him."

Brandy was once again uninterested in the conversation and continued looking around the study, wondering which bookcase was hiding a secret passageway.

"I'm not sure I care to know much about my father," she remarked in a somewhat cold tone, "but I'll keep it in mind."

Brandy ran her fingers through a layer of dust on the desktop and made a face. The thought of cleaning the place without help was almost frightening. Rockwell managed a tiny smile and grimaced.

"The maid has been underperforming since your father's death, I'm afraid," Rockwell informed her.

"Maid?" Brandy asked, feeling some relief at the prospect of someone else doing the dusting.

The rest of that sentence then dawned on her. *Underperforming?* At that moment, the study door opened without warning, revealing a young woman. The maid, Jana, was a short and petite woman in her mid-twenties with long, straight blonde hair that reached midway down her back. Looking more like a woman on her way to a nightclub than a housekeeper, Jana wore heavy makeup, a revealing blouse, and a short leather skirt, showcasing her ample cleavage and voluptuous figure. She appeared surprised to see them and immediately fumbled over herself.

"Oh, forgive me," Jana announced. "I thought I heard voices." She then managed a smile. "I didn't know you were arriving this morning. I'm sorry I didn't hear the bell."

Rockwell smiled pleasantly at the young, attractive woman. "That's my fault, Jana," Attorney Rockwell announced. "The door was unlocked, so I let myself in, but I probably should've knocked." He then looked at Brandy. "Ms. Holloway, this is Jana, the maid." He looked back at Jana. "Jana, this is Ms. Holloway, Mr. Holloway's daughter. She'll be your new employer."

Jana nodded politely.

"Jana has agreed to stay on as long as you need her," Rockwell informed Brandy. "Though I'm afraid the butler has retired."

"If you'd like, I'll serve coffee and pastries in the front sitting room," Jana announced.

"Thank you, Jana," Rockwell replied and watched as Jana scurried from the room. He glanced at Brandy and managed a weak smile. "She's a very nice girl and a hard worker, but she needs a lot of instruction." He drew a breath, then sighed. "Parker, the retired butler, thought you should know that." He glanced at his watch, then at her, and smiled. "Apologize to Jana for me. I have a noon appointment with my wife's attorney." Rockwell grimaced slightly, then appeared almost amused. "I'm sorry I couldn't give you the grand tour, but I'll be back later this afternoon. You can sign the paperwork then. That'll give you plenty of time to look around and familiarize yourself with the mansion and estate grounds."

Once Rockwell left the study, Brandy looked around the room, feeling overwhelmed as well as a little unnerved by it all. She insecurely rubbed her chilled shoulders, although it wasn't even cold in the room. Before deciding what to do first, Brandy texted her mother, asking briefly whether she knew about her half-brother, Ford. After a long pause with no response despite the text having been read, her mother finally texted back that she was in a meeting and would call her later that afternoon. Her mother's non-answer felt like an answer, and Brandy was a little disappointed that her mother never told her about her half-brother. Just one more reason to hate her father even more than she already did.

Chapter 7

Brandy walked along the massive, grand hallway and stared at the medieval weaponry and gothic paintings on the walls. She then eyed each suit of armor she passed. Brandy wasn't sure why, but she felt as if each one was watching her. Just the grand hallway by itself was immense and creepy. She hadn't even ventured into any of the other closed-door rooms, being overwhelmed with the size of the place as it was. She paused in the hallway and looked at the main entrance at the far end, then at the opposite end, which seemed miles away. For a moment, she pondered leaving. How could she stay in a museum-sized house? It was big and intimidating. Not to mention creepy. She again looked around and shivered slightly. Did she mention creepy? It then dawned on her. She had friends who enjoyed creepy things. Brandy removed her cell phone from her pocket and sent a quick group text to her closest friends, inviting them to spend a few nights at the house she'd inherited.

Brandy also asked Eva to pack a bag for her, since it was a long drive and she didn't want to drive back for a few days' worth of clothing. While waiting for a response from her friends, she continued toward the tall, double doors at the far end of the grand hallway that had earlier piqued her curiosity. Brandy wasn't even sure where the kitchen was located or even if she'd ever find Jana again. Brandy was positive the doors at the end of the hall didn't lead to the kitchen, but she just wanted to know what was behind the big, twelve-foot-tall doors. She pushed one of the loudly creaking doors open, possibly opening the gates to hell, and peered inside. Brandy stood in the doorway a moment, staring in awe. Apparently, she found the ballroom. Brandy had never even been in a house that had one. The ballroom was a massive, mostly empty room designed for entertaining large groups of guests. The tall ceiling featured exposed beams, while the black-and-white checkered marble floor was highly glossed, allowing Brandy to see her reflection. The same floor-to-ceiling windows, without curtains, lined the long wall and one of the end walls.

There were old paintings in frilly, antique frames on the walls, a few sideboards, and a couple of antique chairs. Oddly enough, there was an old, black grand piano in the far corner that, despite its age, seemed too modern for the rest of the room. In the opposite corner was a set of life-sized jousting knights on horseback. Brandy was immediately drawn to the display and approached for a closer look. The realistic-looking horses and knights were in full battle armor, complete with jousting poles. The knight horses were either excellent fakes or actual taxidermy horses. As depicted in the stained glass painting on the staircase landing, one horse was white and the other black. A knight in black armor sat upon the black horse, while the one in silver armor rode the white horse. Although they were out in the open, a velvet rope was set up around the display. Despite finding the ballroom somewhat unsettling, at least it wasn't as creepy as the rest of the place. Well, unless the knight horses were taxidermies, then she might reconsider.

Brandy eyed the jousting knights' display once more, then made a hasty exit, not wanting to find out the answer. She left the ballroom and stared at the long, broad grand hallway with all its suits of armor lined along the walls. They were just waiting for her to walk past them again. She wasn't sure why they made her so tense. She knew it was childish, but she didn't want to risk them jumping out at her. When she heard someone rustling around within one of the nearby rooms, Brandy pushed open the swinging door and practically darted inside, finally having found the kitchen. She immediately stopped and looked around the equally creepy kitchen. Brandy muttered a curse under her breath at the almost chilling vibe. The gothic kitchen was large, open, and dark. The black cabinets with gold trim extended up to the fifteen-foot ceiling. There was also a large island counter with a black and mauve marble top, which was at least twelve feet long, with seating for five. The remaining walls had black and purple wallpaper.

Across the kitchen, there was a small alcove with a curved bench seat and a round table with enough seating for six people, if they really liked one another. The bench frame and table were the same black with gold, matching the cabinets, while the wall behind them had black wallpaper with large purple flowers. Jana jumped nervously from Brandy's theatrical entrance and nearly dropped the tray of coffee and cups.

"Sorry, Ms. Holloway," Jana announced and laughed nervously. "It's been so quiet around here lately that I forgot I'm not alone."

"I understand," Brandy replied, knowing how she felt. "This is going to be an adjustment for me as well." If she were being honest, she was just happy to see another living human being. Not that she was scared or anything. "I, uh, invited some of my friends to stay with me for a couple of days. I'm hoping they'll be arriving tomorrow."

"Yes, ma'am," Jana announced, then seemed apprehensive. "Forgive me for asking, but what would you like me to do?" She grimaced slightly. "Parker always gave me instructions. I've been a little lost without him."

Brandy couldn't help but chuckle, feeling the same way. "I could use some additional guidance myself," she replied. "We'll figure it out. If it's no trouble, I'd like to skip that coffee for now. Maybe you could do me a big favor and show me around. I wouldn't want to get lost for several hours." Or be alone, but she wasn't going to mention that.

"Certainly, ma'am," Jana replied, happy with the suggestion.

§

After Jana showed Brandy around the mansion, which took nearly an hour and didn't even include the two basements, Brandy decided to check out the back garden. From what she'd seen from the windows on her tour, it was beautiful and deserved a closer look. She didn't need Jana for that. It wasn't as if she'd get lost in the garden. The mansion was pretty easy to spot from every corner of the estate grounds. The sprawling garden just beyond the pool and patio was well-tended, once upon a time. Although it appeared as if it had been left unattended for a week or more, possibly even before Cullen's death. There were many smaller hedges surrounding the stone walkways and larger areas of blossoming flowers. The walkway circled a beautiful, large water fountain, which seemed to be the garden's focal point. The gray stone fountain was four tiers, with water cascading down each tier into the base, approximately fifteen feet in diameter and more than two feet deep.

There were several marble benches throughout the bright, cheerful, full acre of landscaped lawn. Surprisingly, there weren't any dragon statues or even a hint of anything gothic beyond the mansion walls in the rear estate. Off to the left of the fountain was the only statue, which was a life-sized black marble horse. The horse was standing proudly on a two-foot-tall, marble pedestal, its head arched, its mane and tail seemingly flowing, and one front leg high in the air, as if taking a fighting stance. Definitely a warrior horse of some sort. To the right of the fountain was the gardener's workshop. It was a small, single-story brick building, possibly the size of a three-car garage, maybe it had been the garage in a former life, or even an old carriage house. The building was still intact, but it had seen better days and lacked maintenance. Beyond the gardener's workshop was the eight-bay garage with living quarters on the second floor. The garage maintained the same rustic appeal as the mansion, despite being less than a decade old. It had the same stone exterior with elegant, wooden doors.

Brandy paused before the black marble horse statue and studied it for a long moment. Despite being marble, it was amazingly detailed. She wasn't sure how long she stood there staring at the horse statue before the relaxing sound of the fountain caught her attention. She crossed the garden and approached the fountain. It was quite beautiful, and Brandy thought the marble benches near the fountain would be a great spot to sit and listen to the water. She wasn't sure how long she sat there, looking around the garden and listening to the water. Her mind was cluttered with the mess that her life seemed to have become during the last couple of weeks. She couldn't deny that her father's death, *and life*, crossed her mind more than it should have. Now, she learned she also had a half-brother that she knew nothing about. It was just another reason to feel anger and hatred toward her bastard father. Did his son get the attention he never gave her? Was he a father to his son? What happened that led him to cut his son out of his will? Why did he leave everything to the daughter he never wanted to know?

There were just so many new questions, it was exhausting. She also had a few awkward questions for her mother as well, but that conversation would wait for another day. When she felt hungry, she realized she hadn't eaten all day. Brandy wasn't really sure where the entire afternoon had gone. It had been a bitter-sweet sort of day. She couldn't deny that she loved the mansion and could barely believe that it belonged to her, but considering where it came from, she wasn't sure how she felt about that. Just to add insult to injury, she realized she'd need to raid her father's clothing drawers and at least find something to wear to bed tonight.

Chapter 8

Not only was Jana a poor housekeeper, but her cooking skills were severely lacking as well, making Brandy wonder why her father kept her around in the first place. While casting a quick peek at the young, attractive maid in her revealing clothing, Brandy realized she already knew the answer to that question, but didn't want to entertain it. She wished the butler hadn't quit, since he would have been able to give Brandy more insight and guidance. At the very least, he could have warned her about Jana's cooking. Had she known, Brandy would have gladly prepared something to eat for both of them. She'd have to familiarize herself with the kitchen tomorrow morning and get a jump on breakfast before Jana could attempt it. As if reading her mind or perhaps after watching Brandy pick at her meal, Jana felt the need to say something.

"I'm not really a good cook," Jana informed her while grimacing. "Parker did most of the cooking. He was a pretty talented chef."

"I wasn't actually all that hungry," Brandy easily lied. "I'm sure the food is fine."

"You're being too kind," Jana replied while offering a tiny, humored smile. "On the bright side, the pantry is filled with junk food, and the freezer is stocked with plenty of ice cream."

"I'll keep that in mind for later this evening," Brandy announced.

A strange clanging sound startled Brandy. Jana immediately perked up and eyed her new employer.

"That's the front door," Jana informed her. "I guess Attorney Rockwell made it back sooner than anticipated."

When Jana made a motion to move out from behind the island counter, Brandy jumped off her pub chair.

"It's okay, Jana," Brandy announced. "I'll get it. He's here to see me anyway."

Brandy left the kitchen and headed down the grand hallway, casting sideways glances at every suit of armor as she passed. At least she knew how to reach the foyer, although it was quite the trek from the kitchen. No wonder Parker retired. Even at a brisk walk, it seemed to take Brandy forever to reach the foyer. She opened the door without even looking through the peephole. It wasn't as if any solicitors were making the long drive to the mansion, and even if they did, they'd take one look at the place and turn tail. When she saw her mother standing in the doorway, Brandy couldn't deny she was a little stunned.

"Mom--?" Brandy gasped, surprised. "I wasn't expecting you to come all the way out here."

Nadia managed a tiny smile, although she seemed uncomfortable. "Your text blindsided me a little," she announced almost timidly. "I thought this should be a face-to-face conversation." She then cringed. "Can I come in?"

Brandy practically jumped out of the doorway. "Of course," she announced. "You're my mother. You don't even have to ask."

When Nadia entered and barely batted a lash at the interior, Brandy immediately knew her mother had been in the house before. Once she closed the door, Brandy and her mother walked down the foyer steps together. Brandy glanced to either side of the grand hallway, trying to figure out which was the formal sitting room and which was the library, not that it mattered, since both had sofas. Nadia cringed slightly and pointed to the left. Brandy groaned softly and shook her head, ashamed that she still didn't know which room was where.

"Did you live here with him before I was born?" Brandy finally asked as she led her mother into the front sitting room.

"Two years, actually," her mother replied, seeming almost nostalgic.

The formal living room, or front sitting room, was a sea of dark purple. Being a corner room, on two of the four walls, it had four, floor-to-ceiling windows with long purple curtains tied back with purple and silver nylon cord, and grayish-colored walls. A massive purple-and-gold throw rug covered almost the entire floor. Two large, purple tapestry sofas were on either side of a large, black leather coffee table. Two oversized armchairs near the double doors were also covered in purple fabric, as were the two smaller purple upholstered chairs with intricate black frames in front of the massive black fireplace. The marble fireplace was beautifully hand-carved and amazingly detailed. Rather than a painting above the fireplace mantel, which was covered in candlesticks, there was a large mirror built into the wall. There were two other mirrors along the inside wall, with small tables and decorative lamps with purple fabric shades. The light from the candles and lamps would reflect off the mirrors, creating an even brighter room. Nadia looked around the room before sitting on the closest sofa.

"I always loved this room," Nadia remarked with a contented sigh.

"Your favorite color is purple," Brandy announced, then managed a tiny laugh. "The color scheme suddenly makes sense."

"Actually," her mother began. "The rooms were these colors long before I lived here. That they're purple is only a coincidence."

Brandy sat at the far end of the same sofa, facing her mother. "I have so many questions," she announced.

"I know," Nadia replied with a defeated sigh. "Where would you like to start?"

"Obviously, you knew my father was rich," Brandy remarked. "I get why you didn't feel it was necessary to mention it. Attorney Rockwell explained how my father took care of us financially, but I don't understand why you didn't at least warn me about what I was walking into here. You knew I was meeting with his lawyer. All of this was quite a shock."

"I know," Nadia replied while frowning. "But I really wasn't expecting him to leave you his estate. I assumed he'd leave you money but not the house. If I knew you were driving all the way out here to meet with the lawyer, I would have warned you."

"Considering I'd never even met my biological father, it makes sense that you wouldn't think he'd leave me his house," Brandy remarked. "I have to assume he left the estate to me to keep it from going to his son." Brandy eyed her mother. "That's the bigger conversation. Why didn't you tell me I had a half-brother?"

"That was long before your father met me," Nadia informed her. "I'd never even met Ford."

"So he abandoned his son as well, huh?" Brandy asked.

"We never spoke about his son," Nadia reported, seeming uncomfortable. "He didn't even have any pictures of him that I'd seen. Since I'd never met him and never heard anything about him, I didn't see a reason to mention him to you." She shifted on the sofa and gently cleared her throat. "I hope you're not mad at me, but I didn't want to complicate your life or give you reason to hate your father more than you already did."

"No, I'm not mad at you, Mom," Brandy replied with a deep sigh. "I was just a little blindsided by the news. I wish I had heard it from you and not Cullen's lawyer."

Nadia finally smiled, relieved. "I'm glad you aren't upset," she announced and finally relaxed. "I was a little worried."

"If you're actually worried," Brandy remarked while hiding her smile. "You can stay the night and keep me company."

"I'd love to," her mother announced, then cringed. "But I have an important meeting in the morning. I can come back tomorrow night, if you'd like the company."

"You're more than welcome," Brandy informed her. "But, just so you know, my friends will be here."

Nadia's smile suddenly faded. "Clair and Randall?" she asked.

"Yes, they'll be here too."

"I'll come for a couple of nights after your friends are gone," Nadia informed her. "Randall and his antique sales pitches are a bit much for me. He's either trying to buy things I don't want to sell or trying to sell me stuff I don't want to buy. I can only handle him in small doses."

Both hesitated, then looked around the front sitting room, cringing simultaneously. Randall was going to be like a kid in a candy store in Brandy's new gothic museum.

"Oh, it's going to be a long weekend," Brandy moaned softly.

"He's going to be out of his mind," Nadia remarked.

"I hadn't really thought that through, had I?" Brandy groaned.

Nadia cringed and shook her head.

Chapter 9

By the time Attorney Rockwell arrived two hours later, Brandy's mother was almost ready to leave. When Nadia smiled politely at Rockwell, Brandy was almost certain her mother had met him before, despite what Rockwell said earlier. Perhaps it was during their divorce, which would be a sore subject for her mother, and Brandy wasn't about to ask.

"We'll only be about an hour," Rockwell announced to Brandy. "If your mother wants to wait until we're finished--"

"No," Nadia announced, answering for herself. "I should be heading out if I want to get back home before dark." She then looked at her daughter. "If you don't mind, I'd like to take a quick walk around the property before heading out."

"Of course," Brandy replied. "Take your time. Check the place out. Just don't get lost."

"I won't," Nadia replied with a soft chuckle. "I'll call you in a couple of days about coming up to stay."

Nadia and Brandy exchanged farewell hugs before Brandy headed into the study with Rockwell. Once Rockwell closed the door behind them, Nadia turned and hurried up the grand staircase with a mission in mind. The second floor hallway had the same carpeting as the grand stairs and covered the entire area. The corridor, circling the whole floor from the right stairs to the left stairs, was approximately eight feet wide and had a twelve-foot-tall, rich mahogany ceiling with decorative trim. Smaller, simple chandeliers were spaced every twenty feet along the length of the hallway. The walls were covered in crimson and black velvet wallpaper, creating a moderately dark, somewhat creepy atmosphere. There were several carved antique tables and chairs along the hallway, as well as the occasional painting on the walls. Each of the ten bedrooms had beautifully rich mahogany doors, old-fashioned copper fixtures, and elegantly carved doorframes.

Quickly and quietly, Nadia approached the master bedroom and slipped inside. She stopped just inside the room, shutting the door behind her, and paused, taking in the old, familiar room. The master bedroom was approximately seven hundred square feet with a tongue-and-groove hardwood floor, while the walls and ceiling were the same rich mahogany as the hallway. There were four, floor-to-ceiling, rounded stained-glass windows along the outer wall as well as the matching balcony doors. A magnificent, black and gray marble fireplace took up most of the far wall across from the foot end of the bed. The furniture was a heavy Victorian antique, containing violet marble tops, with the crowning jewel of the room being the tall, king-sized hardtop canopy bed. The carved detail of the wooden canopy was breathtaking. The high headboard was a mix of black leather and carved wood. Not surprisingly, the detailed headboard was a massive, carved dragon. Smaller dragons were carved on all four pillar-style bedposts, seemingly spiraling up each column.

What stuck out most in the master bedroom was the use of black and purple decor. The bed had dark purple pillows and bedspread; the window curtains were also dark purple, and the couch, chair, and bench at the foot of the bed were either purple or black leather. The overall vibe was somewhat creepy, keeping in theme with the rest of the house. There was no telling which memories Nadia was reliving in that moment. Whichever, they were short-lived. Nadia hurried across the bedroom toward the tall bed, continuing on her mission. She ran her hand along the headboard, hesitated, and pushed on a panel. The panel popped open, and she eagerly looked inside. To her horror, the compartment was empty. Nadia's expression dropped as concern swept over her.

"No," she whispered.

A shadow loomed over her, and she was immediately aware of someone's presence. She hesitated, then spun around. Nadia's eyes widened as she suddenly cried out.

§

Once Rockwell had all the paperwork laid out on the elegant desktop, he stood and indicated for Brandy to sit at the desk. She was slightly reluctant but did as he instructed. He handed her his gold pen while hovering over her shoulder and explained everything she was signing. Brandy took her time reading the papers before signing them. It wasn't that she didn't trust him, but she just didn't trust him. She also didn't like him hovering over her shoulder. That same ominous feeling crept over her with Rockwell standing so close. She couldn't even describe the feeling or why she was feeling ill at ease with him so close. It wasn't as if he was flirting or even touching her. When Jana brought coffee into the study, Brandy was relieved for the interruption. Unfortunately, it also prolonged Attorney Rockwell's visit.

"Did you explore the mansion this afternoon?" Rockwell asked from across the desk while they took a break and drank coffee.

"Jana showed me around," Brandy replied, then hesitated before reluctantly responding. "Well, everything except the two basements."

"The one off the kitchen is pretty rough," Rockwell informed her. "You probably wouldn't appreciate its condition. It's rather dark and dingy down there. I could give you a tour of the front basement. The wine cellar and cigar lounge are incredible."

Despite wanting to see the finished basement, particularly while not alone, Brandy wasn't too keen on spending more time with Rockwell. She was worried hanging around him would uncover whatever sixth sense she was having about him.

"Actually, it's been a long, tiring day," Brandy informed him, which wasn't a lie. "I think I'd rather just take a bath, crawl under the covers, and read a book."

"That's understandable," Rockwell replied, then indicated the papers on her desk. "Why don't we get the rest of those papers signed, and I can leave you to your peaceful evening?"

"I'd appreciate that."

§

After finding a book in the vast library, Brandy staked her claim in the master bedroom. To say she was a little uncomfortable in the room that formerly belonged to her father was an understatement. Yet here she was, rummaging through his closet, plucking one of *his* button-down dress shirts from a hanger to wear as a nightshirt to sleep in *his* bed. The whole thing made her about as uncomfortable as she could possibly get, but she kept reminding herself that it was now her house. She never even met her father. She just needed to forget he'd ever lived there, and after she got over the initial creep factor, she could make it work. Heaving herself onto the excessively tall bed was a bit of an effort, which would be compounded when she needed to get up and go to the bathroom in the middle of the night. Brandy sat on the bed and tried to read her borrowed book from the downstairs library, but the large, open bedroom made her somewhat restless. She had gotten used to her cozy, phone booth-sized room in her apartment. The sheer size of the master bedroom was almost intimidating and a bit unnerving.

Despite her unease in the large space, the bed was surprisingly comfortable, and the house seemed blissfully quiet. It was actually nice not hearing her upstairs neighbors thumping around above her head. Brandy hesitated and looked around. Of course, maybe it was too quiet. She tried to sink into her book to take her mind off how quiet and creepy the house was. Despite the quietness, she heard the occasional creaking sounds from the mansion's interior. Every so often, the sounds echoed softly. Her mind then strayed from her book, leaving her curious about the sound and exactly where it was coming from. Amidst the silence, Brandy suddenly heard a woman's faint yet shrill scream from somewhere deep inside the house, possibly coming from the first floor. When she heard the faint bloodcurdling scream again, Brandy tossed her book aside, sprang from the bed, and ran from the room. She ran down the second floor hallway toward the back stairs that would take her to the kitchen, surprisingly finding them rather quickly, and thundered down them.

"Jana!"

Brandy ran into the dimly lit kitchen, skidded to a stop in her bare feet, and looked around, panting heavily from her sprint and fright.

"Jana!"

Jana ran into the kitchen from the adjoining servant's wing and appeared alarmed. "What is it, Ms. Holloway?" she gasped while looking around. "Is something wrong?"

Brandy stared at Jana in stunned disbelief. "I heard you scream," she cried out. "What happened?"

"I didn't scream," Jana insisted, looking bewildered and only briefly eyeing her in Cullen's dress shirt as a nightgown.

"I heard a woman scream," Brandy insisted, now turning defensive.

"Sorry, ma'am, but I didn't hear anything," Jana informed her.

How was it possible that Jana didn't hear anything? She was on the first floor where the scream almost certainly originated. More importantly, how was it possible that the woman screaming hadn't been Jana?

Jana suddenly seemed visibly uncomfortable and shifted. "Although--" she remarked, then hesitated. "I don't know if I should say anything."

"What is it?" Brandy asked, quickly becoming frustrated after her fright and brisk run through half the house.

Jana appeared concerned and looked around the room, as if afraid someone else might be listening. "I'm convinced this house is haunted," she whispered. "Parker told me never to mention it to anyone, but you have a right to know."

"Haunted?" Brandy asked, surprised.

Jana sounded a little crazy, but Brandy wasn't ready to completely doubt her theory just yet. After all, look at the house! Even Norman Bates would be uncomfortable here.

"I'm sorry," Jana announced, becoming flustered. "I've upset you."

"No, no, not at all," Brandy replied, finally recovering from her sprint and fear that someone had been mutilating poor Jana. "You've heard screams before?"

"Not screams, but strange things have happened around here, more so since Mr. Holloway died," Jana insisted, then hesitated as her eyes widened. "I've seen *things.*"

"What sort of things?"

"Well, a couple of nights ago, I felt a cold hand on my shoulder," Jana informed her. "When I turned around, there was no one there. There wasn't even anyone else in the house." She shivered slightly and rubbed her chilled arms. "Sometimes, I swear I hear someone walking around down here, but there's never anyone here."

Brandy stared at her a moment longer, feeling apprehensive before regaining her composure. Jana's story didn't sound logical, despite the mansion's haunting vibe.

"I'm not sure I'm ready to believe ghosts are haunting this place," Brandy remarked, then attempted to dismiss what she'd heard. "It's been a long day, and I'm probably overly tired. Perhaps I was just hearing things."

"I wouldn't make up such things," Jana insisted almost defensively.

"I'm sure you wouldn't," Brandy replied, then managed a tiny smile. "Sorry for waking you."

Chapter 10

Two o'clock in the morning. Despite saying she didn't believe in ghosts, Brandy slept with her bedside lamp and the television on, keeping the room partially lit. With the television volume just loud enough to hear the program, Brandy was comforted by the sound. Even though she had been exhausted, she didn't even attempt to sleep until midnight when she could no longer keep her eyes open. She considered turning on all the bedroom lights, but that seemed like overkill. It didn't matter anyway because her eyes automatically opened every twenty or thirty minutes. A few times, disorientation from being in an unfamiliar place, particularly a bedroom the size of a parking lot, led to confusion. When she did sleep, her nightmares were out of control and wreaking havoc on her sleep. Brandy tossed under the covers of the exceptionally large and comfortable bed. All her nightmares tonight seemed to have one common theme. In each dream, her mother was brutally attacked in front of her, and there was nothing she could do to stop the man from killing her.

Brandy's eyes suddenly popped open after a particularly disturbing nightmare where her mother died at the hands of her father, even though she'd never even seen a picture of her father. As she looked beyond the lighted area surrounding her bed, she swore she saw a man standing in the darkened corner of the room. Brandy gasped and shot up in bed, staring across the room, but there was no one there. What she mistook for a man was possibly a statue on a tall pedestal. She wasn't sure how long she stared across the room before raking trembling fingers through her hair and finally getting out of bed. It had taken her a few minutes to remember where she was, being slightly disoriented in the unfamiliar room. She turned on another table lamp, bringing more light to the room, which helped her relax a little. Brandy then walked to the glass balcony doors and looked outside into the night. The moon was nearly full, brightening the estate grounds enough to see fairly clearly. Brandy opened the doors, walked onto the terrace, and leaned on the railing.

The slightly cooler night breeze felt good, considering how warm she had been from thrashing beneath the covers. The countryside seemed so peaceful, yet she felt full of angst. She looked at the elegant garden, having the perfect fountain view from her room. The moonlight practically glistened off the lightly erupting water, creating tranquil sounds. Brandy then looked across the garden to the horse statue, but it was gone! She straightened while staring in horror at the empty marble base. She scanned the garden, wondering if she'd been mistaken about its placement, but she didn't see it anywhere. Where would it have gone? How could someone possibly have moved it? Despite her concern, she wasn't about to venture outside in the middle of the night looking for trouble. She'd investigate tomorrow morning. Tonight, she'd remain locked in her room.

Early the following morning, as the sun rose, Brandy woke to warm sunlight touching her face. She attempted to open her tired, heavy eyes, having some difficulty due to exhaustion. She stared at the stained glass window only a couple of feet from her face, taking a moment to remember where she was. Brandy slowly turned over in the heavy comforter wrapped around her, where she had been sleeping in the deep garden tub. Yes, it was somewhat childish; a grown woman being afraid while alone in the massive bedroom, but the bathroom was a much smaller, cozier room. As she sat up with the comforter still partially covering her while inside the tub, she looked across the bathroom at the door, which she'd barricaded with the smaller antique chair from the master bedroom. Okay, maybe she took her paranoia a little too far last night, but at least she got some sleep. It wasn't as if anyone would ever know.

The large bathroom was a masterpiece of beauty and a symbol of wealth. The cream-colored tile was outlined with smaller dark brown tiles in a diamond pattern, creating an intricate design in the center of the twenty-foot-by-twenty-foot area between the two sink vanities. A large chandelier hung from the vaulted ceiling, high above the center of the room. In a separate alcove, the sunken garden tub sat before the large stained-glass window. On either side of the tub were frosted shower doors to the walk-through shower, completely encased in tile, with bench seating, multiple shower heads, and the back of the tub's stained-glass window lining up with the outside stained-glass window.

In her quest to make sure no one knew about last night's sleeping arrangements, Brandy crawled out of the tub and dragged the massive comforter back to the bedroom along with the small chair. Before taking her shower, she made the bed, putting the comforter back in place, where it belonged. Brandy had to admit her favorite thing about the mansion was her new bathroom. She spent a little extra time in the walk-through shower, allowing all eight showerheads douse her at once with hot water. Initially, it seemed weird being naked in what felt like a stone hallway with water shooting at her from every angle, but she soon realized how much she enjoyed it. Although the window to the outside was beveled and stained glass, it was still quite exhilarating to have a window in her shower. Despite having to wear her undergarments and shorts from the previous day, she borrowed another of her father's button-down shirts for something clean to wear. As soon as she was shower-fresh and ready for her day, Brandy had to take care of the first thing on her to-do list.

§

Brandy hurried along the garden path, past the fountain, and to the missing horse statue. She immediately stopped when she saw that the horse statue was once again proudly displayed upon its pedestal. Brandy stared at the statue for several minutes in silent disbelief. She hadn't been imagining it. Or had she? She scanned the remainder of the garden, then approached the statue for a closer look, not caring if she crushed any flowers along the way. She firmly patted the solid marble. There was no way that statue could have been moved without a crane. She had to have been imagining it!

§

Rather than risking another horrible meal, Brandy decided to make breakfast before Jana had a chance. Before she started breakfast, she leaned across the massive island counter and texted her mother. Brandy couldn't deny her nightmares about her mother dying many times and in many gruesome ways had played on her mind even after the sun was up. She wanted to text her last night at two in the morning, but she knew her mother would be worried sick with a middle-of-the-night rant. Only a few minutes after she'd sent the text, her mother texted back, confirming that she was fine and would be in meetings all morning. When asked if she wanted her to call later after her meetings, Brandy responded that it was okay, and she'd call her in a couple of days after her friends left. Brandy then went about making breakfast. She made scrambled eggs, bacon, and toast. Possibly the smell of brewing coffee drew Jana to the kitchen from the staff wing. Although dressed and ready to start her day, Jana appeared a little bewildered.

"I would have made breakfast, Ms. Holloway," Jana informed her.

"I was already up," Brandy replied with a smile that quite possibly gave away her true motive for making breakfast.

Jana didn't pursue the conversation further because she knew she was a bad cook. No one had to tell her. The young woman felt a little uncomfortable sitting at the island counter with her boss while they had breakfast together, but the awkwardness quickly passed.

"How did you sleep in your new quarters?" Jana asked while sipping her coffee. "I hope the room temperature was satisfactory. Mr. Holloway usually kept the rooms a little cooler."

"The room was fine," Brandy replied, then carefully worded her response about how she slept. She certainly wasn't going to tell Jana she slept in the bathtub with the door barricaded. "The bed was comfortable, but I always have some trouble sleeping the first night in a new place."

"I could have the florist deliver some lavender flowers for your room," Jana informed her. "Lavender is very soothing."

"I'll be fine," Brandy replied. "But thanks for the offer."

She'd be fine because her friends would be coming today, and she wouldn't feel as if she were in the big, creepy mansion all by herself.

§

Brandy let Jana handle breakfast cleanup and found her way to the study. It was time to see what she could dig up on the mansion, even if it meant learning some things about her father from his journal. She sat behind the desk and opened several drawers, thoroughly rummaging through them. When her cell phone dinged, indicating she had a text, she checked the message, assuming it was from one of her friends. Instead, it was from an unknown number. The message was from a temp agency that simply stated Attorney Rockwell asked them to send her a temporary house manager to facilitate her transition. She could later decide whether to keep him, replace him, or go without assistance. Brandy was a little surprised that someone would be over that afternoon, but she was grateful and a little relieved. She didn't know how she'd have a stress-free visit with her friends while keeping an eye on Jana.

Brandy resumed rummaging through the desk drawers on her quest with renewed hope. When she didn't find what she was looking for in the desk, she moved to the closest bookcase and pulled out each book before slamming it back into place as her frustration increased. Jana appeared in the open study doorway and watched her for a moment before finally speaking.

"Can I help you find something, Ms. Holloway?" Jana asked.

Brandy looked at Jana in the doorway, slightly startled, and then relaxed. "Rockwell told me my father had kept a journal," she informed her. "It was supposed to be in the desk, but it's not there. I thought maybe I'd try the bookshelf. Had you seen his journal?"

"I don't remember seeing a journal, but I'll keep an eye out for it," Jana remarked, then seemed to lose interest. "I finished cleaning up from breakfast. Can I get you anything before I take my break?"

"No, thanks," Brandy replied, then looked up, discontinuing her search for a moment. "Oh, Jana, the agency is sending a new butler here sometime today. I guess he'll need a room."

"Oh," Jana replied with some surprise. "I didn't know you were replacing Parker so soon."

"It was a little sudden, but the agency texted me and said Rockwell recommended they send someone over," Brandy replied. "I'm sure with my friends coming, you could use the extra help."

Jana appeared uneasy but managed a smile. "That's very kind of you, Ms. Holloway," she replied. "I could use the help."

"It may be just temporary," Brandy informed her while remaining preoccupied. "I'm not sure what I want to do long term."

"Of course," Jana replied. "I'll freshen Parker's old room before I take my break."

Chapter 11

Later that morning, Brandy entered the mansion's library, which was bigger and taller than one of the rooms at her mother's art gallery. The main level had a set of glass doors leading out to the terrace, while the built-in bookshelves encompassed the rest of the wall space, excluding the small section occupied by the stone fireplace. Several rolling ladders reached higher shelves, while a series of leather sofas, comfortable chairs with ottomans, end tables, and coffee tables occupied the center of the room. A spiral wrought-iron ladder ascended to the second floor, which was just a single row of bookcases circling the entire room. The same decorative wrought iron was used for the railing on the second level, giving the room an airy cathedral-ceiling feel. Brandy clung to the rolling ladder and rummaged through several old books on the top shelf. Surprisingly, she had already checked every title on the lower shelves on the right side of the library. Her frustration was increasing with each old book she opened that wasn't her father's journal. It was going to take forever!

When she felt someone place their cold hand on her bare leg, she just about fell off the ladder, startled. Brandy jerked with a gasp and looked behind her. There wasn't anyone in the library, and she was still alone. She involuntarily shuddered and rubbed her leg, still feeling the chilling phantom touch. Was she going insane? The house certainly couldn't be haunted as Jana had suggested. Could it? Brandy finally relaxed and pulled another old book from the shelf. She nearly dropped the book but caught it, opening it by accident. Within the dusty pages was a drawing depicting a medieval torture method. Brandy grimaced at the graphic drawing and was about to shut the book when a droplet of blood spattered on the page. Brandy withheld her gasp and immediately looked up. A dark pool of blood had soaked through the high, vaulted first floor ceiling and dripped again, a droplet striking the book's page.

Brandy gasped and dropped the book, which clattered to the floor. She just about jumped down the ladder, almost falling, and ran to the library stairs. When she looked up to the second floor ceiling, before making the climb, she saw a massive area soaked with blood. It was coming from the third floor! Since there was no access to the second floor hallway from the library's upper level, Brandy had to take the grand stairs to the third floor. She sprinted out the library doors, ran across the grand hallway, swung the staircase banister, and bolted up the steps straight to the third floor staircase, entering the empty artist's room. Brandy looked around the large, vacant room directly above the second floor library, seeing absolutely nothing. It wasn't possible! Brandy heard the doorbell as she ran down the third floor stairs, but dismissed it. She needed to figure out where the blood came from.

Brandy thundered down the main staircase to the first floor and rushed past Jana, who stood before the open front door. Jana practically whirled around and watched her employer run back to the library. Brandy entered the library and looked up. The pool of blood on the ceiling was gone! As she stared at the ceiling, she questioned her sanity once more. Did she really just imagine that?

"Ms. Holloway, is something wrong?" Jana asked from the library doorway.

Brandy snatched the discarded book from the floor and leafed through it, looking for the blood-smeared page, too distracted to look back at Jana.

"Uh, no," she replied as she continued leafing through the book.

"Ms. Holloway, this is Raven," Jana announced. "The new butler from the agency."

Brandy barely looked up, just about noticing the neatly dressed man standing behind Jana, and didn't acknowledge him.

"That was fast," Brandy remarked, then looked back at the ceiling.

The new butler entered the room, approached Brandy near the ladder, and tilted his head while looking at the ceiling as well before finally clearing his throat.

"Where would you like me to start, madam?" he asked in a refined English accent.

Brandy immediately turned, having heard the accent and realizing he was now only a few feet from her. "I'm sorry," she announced and got her first look at him.

Raven appeared to be in his late twenties to early thirties and stood an imposing six foot two, with a somewhat muscular build that was almost hidden beneath his black suit, black dress shirt, and black tie. Undeniably handsome, he had short dark hair that was more modern than traditional with that freshly 'fingers run through' look. Although he was currently clean-shaven, his five o'clock shadow was already showing, and it wasn't even late morning yet. For a servant, he had an unusually commanding and almost superior air about him. Brandy stared at Raven for a moment, surprised that he was a younger, handsome man. A tiny, embarrassed smile crossed her face, and she hoped she didn't blush.

"I didn't mean to be rude," Brandy remarked, then pointed at the ceiling. "It's just--" She hesitated and quickly waved it off. "Never mind."

"Will you be needing anything else, Ms. Holloway?" Jana asked.

"Uh, no, thank you, Jana."

Jana stepped out of the room, eyed the new butler, and then closed the door behind her. Brandy fidgeted slightly while simultaneously taking in an eyeful of the handsome man.

"I'm, uh, rather new at this employer thing," Brandy informed him while remaining tense. "I'm, uh, expecting some weekend guests tonight, and I don't want to worry about anything while they're here."

"That's why I'm here, madam," Raven insisted while adding a tiny, knowing smile. "I'll take care of everything." He then appeared curious. "How many guests are you expecting?"

"Five total," Brandy informed him. "Two or three tonight, and the rest tomorrow."

"How many guestrooms?" he asked. "One for each?"

"Uh, no," Brandy replied. "Just four."

"I'll see that four guestrooms are freshened and speak to Jana about dinner," Raven informed her.

"That would be wonderful," Brandy replied and finally released the tense breath she'd been holding. "Although it might be best if we ordered dinner out." She cringed slightly. "It's just, well, Jana--"

"The agency gave me the retired butler's contact information," Raven informed her while offering an oddly knowing look. "I've been thoroughly briefed on

Jana's employment qualifications." He cocked his head while studying her. "Part of my job is overseeing the rest of the staff, and I feel you should know, my standards are a little higher than Jana might be used to."

"You saw the dust, huh?" Brandy remarked, then grimaced.

"No, madam," he announced. "I can *smell* the dust, and I'm not holding out much hope for the kitchen either."

"I understand," Brandy replied, almost feeling intimidated by Raven herself. She kind of felt bad for what Jana was about to face. "Just don't do anything drastic like fire her before my friends arrive without a backup plan."

"That won't be a problem," Raven replied. "She'll be given a probation period before that happens." He offered an oddly charming smile. "Everything will be as it should be for your friends' arrival."

Brandy nodded, feeling relieved and anxious at the same time. Raven was about to give Jana a rude awakening. There was an awkward moment of silence as they stared at each other. Brandy couldn't help but admire his handsome features while simultaneously wondering why he was staring at her. Was he waiting for something?

"Will there be anything else, madam?" Raven finally asked, breaking the silence.

Brandy fidgeted and managed a tiny smile. "I don't really know," she asked, then tilted her head. "Should there be?"

There was another awkward moment of silence between them.

"Shall I dismiss myself?" Raven then asked.

Brandy could feel her cheeks turning red, embarrassed that she hadn't realized she needed to dismiss him.

"Uh, sure," she replied, then fidgeted. "I don't mean any disrespect, but I, uh, was actually expecting someone much, well, older."

"I'm older than I look," Raven casually replied and offered a hint of a smile.

Raven gave a slight bow, then headed for the door. Brandy couldn't resist staring after him until he was gone. Her friends would love him, and that could be a big problem.

§

A little after one o'clock that afternoon, an older maroon sports car drove slowly past the mansion and pulled up to the detached eight-car garage. A young woman got out of the car and admired the massive garage. Brandy's friend, Jill, was the typical fresh-faced girl-next-door with shoulder-length blonde hair and hazel eyes. The young woman in her early twenties stood about five-foot-five with a lean to athletic build. Jill eyed the side kitchen door not far from where she parked. She grabbed her overnight bag and headed in that direction. She was about to walk up the few steps to the smaller porch when she heard a small child crying. Jill hesitated, walked away from the porch, and followed the sound to the old gardener's workshop not far from the garage. The workshop appeared untouched for a long time. Jill paused before the door that was ajar and slowly pushed it open.

"Hello?"

Jill stood in the doorway as light filtered into the cluttered workshop filled with work counters, lawn tools, and machinery. More tools of all varieties hung on the back wall, while filled shelves occupied the wall to the left. Despite the reasonably cared-for lawn, the gardener's workshop appeared untouched for possibly years. Of course, most wealthy people hired lawn care services rather than paying a full-time employee. The crying was a little louder.

"Hello?"

Jill slowly entered while looking around the dingy, cobweb-filled workshop. The child's crying was now only sporadic. Jill uncertainly walked deeper into the workshop.

"Little girl? I won't hurt you," Jill called out. "Where are you?"

She saw something that appeared to be a small child run and hide within the dark back corner behind the workbench. Jill slowly approached the large workbench and lowered herself to one knee. The area behind the bench was dark and narrow. The crying instantly stopped. Jill strained to see behind the bench, leaning in closer. She then heard a beastly snarl. Jill's expression turned to horror, and she screamed as something rushed toward her.

Chapter 12

Brandy hurried into the kitchen and found Raven polishing a set of crystal glasses while Jana peeled potatoes. Raven immediately snapped to attention when alerted to her presence, but Jana kept her head down and barely acknowledged her. Raven might have already laid down the law, especially since Jana had recently changed into a less revealing shirt and seemed to be pouting.

"Did you hear that?" Brandy asked while looking at both.

"Hear what, madam?" Raven asked.

"It sounded like a woman screaming," Brandy insisted.

Jana suddenly looked up with surprise, as if reliving last night, and then returned to her potatoes without comment.

"Shall I have a look around?" Raven asked.

Brandy looked at Jana, who continued to work, but she could tell by her body language what she was thinking. It was last night all over again.

"No," Brandy muttered while frowning. "It was probably my imagination again."

When the front doorbell rang, Raven casually set his cloth down and left the kitchen. Brandy stared at Jana a moment longer, somewhat concerned that she still hadn't looked up, and then hurried after Raven. It was a long sprint down the grand hallway, and Brandy still didn't know how Raven got there so fast. Raven stood alongside the open door as Eva and Paula entered the foyer. Paula looked around the impressive yet spine-chilling mansion, unable to hide her grin, while Eva appeared more interested in Raven. When Brandy approached the foyer, Eva and Paula cried out, ran to her, and exchanged squeals and hugs.

"I can't believe this place!" Paula exclaimed. "It's deliciously eerie!"

"You must be so excited," Eva remarked and again gazed at the handsome butler.

"I'm so glad you could make it," Brandy announced, then leaned in closer. "This place has been seriously creeping me out."

Eva immediately pulled Brandy aside. "You have a butler?" she gasped, shifting her gaze again to Raven. "He's gorgeous. Where did you find him?"

"Dial-a-butler," Brandy teased.

"You lucky girl," Eva groaned.

Paula snuck up behind them and leaned over their shoulders. "Can I borrow Jeeves tonight for my bubble bath?" she asked.

"Raven's off-limits, guys," Brandy insisted while attempting to keep her voice down. "Don't scare him away."

"She's already staked her claim," Eva remarked and deviously raised her brows.

Paula once more looked around the mansion, then looked back at Brandy. "So where's Jill?"

"She's not here yet," Brandy replied.

"She should have been here by now," Paula insisted. "She texted and said she was leaving before we did."

"She's probably lost again," Eva muttered while shaking her head.

"I hope not," Brandy remarked. "The back roads around here seem to go on forever without any sign of life."

"She always finds her way," Eva replied, then shrugged. "Eventually." She then turned cheerful. "How about some drinks?

Raven approached as if on cue. "Shall I serve drinks in the game room or the lounge?"

Eva and Paula nearly gave themselves whiplash looking back at Raven the moment they heard the English accent.

"Hmm," Eva cooed. "I love the accent."

"The game room would be terrific," Brandy replied. "Thanks, Raven."

Raven smiled politely at Eva and Paula, indicating for them to follow him. "This way, madams," he announced almost too suavely.

The moment his back was turned, Eva and Paula looked at Brandy and groaned before hurrying after the swiftly moving butler. Brandy held her breath. It was going to be a long weekend keeping her friends in line around Raven. She didn't need him filing sexual harassment charges against her friends, and she certainly didn't want him quitting after only one weekend. Brandy joined her friends in the game room for a drink. After the day she was having, she needed one--or two. Brandy's friends were in awe over what had to be the best room in the house. The game room was easily double the size of Brandy's entire apartment. The walls were the same rich wood as most of the house as were the floor-to-wall windows, which also had a set of double glass doors leading to the outside. An elegant, heavy pool table was nestled against the back wall, not far from the oval, eight-person, felt-top poker table with leather rolling chairs surrounding it. Two sets of pub tables were against the wall, not far from the gaming section.

Closer to the outer doors was a large, eight-person sunken hot tub, offering a perfect view of the garden. On the opposite side of the room was a semi-circular, carved wooden bar with a light marble top and ten stools. Raven headed behind the bar and almost looked at home playing bartender. On the wall behind the bar were decorative shelves filled with top-shelf alcohol, a sink, a small refrigerator, and a large television mounted high on the wall. There was a small living room section to the side of the bar with a leather sofa, a love seat, two chairs, and a large coffee table in the middle. Another large screen television was mounted on the wall near the living area. The game room also had its own massive, walk-in stone fireplace with a marble mantel. Once Paula had her drink, she gravitated to the partially sunken hot tub and ran her finger along the edge while admiring it. She spun, smiled, and sat on the edge.

"I could get used to this life," Paula announced before raising her glass.

Once she had her drink, Eva was finally able to take her eyes off the handsome English butler and approached the poker table.

"When the others get here, there's going to be some poker happening," Eva announced, then glanced at Raven behind the bar while he fixed a drink for Brandy. "Are you in, Raven?"

Raven eyed Eva and smiled, but didn't respond either way. Brandy groaned softly and sat on one of the tall chairs before the bar while watching Raven fix her drink. Raven's allure went well beyond physical features. Brandy often felt invincible to the charm of handsome men; Eva's parade of mythological gods made that abundantly clear, but she couldn't seem to resist whatever it was Raven had going for him. It had been a long time since she ravished a man with her eyes. Actually, not since high school. Perhaps it was the endless sea of artists her mother had in and out of the art gallery that led to her high resistance to handsome men. Brandy shifted uncomfortably on her chair for several reasons, but she felt she needed to address the most important issue at hand.

"If my friends say or do anything you feel is out of line," Brandy began somewhat delicately. "Feel free to tell them off."

Raven briefly glanced up as he finished making her cocktail, offered a hint of a smile, and then placed her drink on the bar before her, finally meeting her gaze.

"I'm not easily offended," Raven casually informed her. "And I'd never deprive houseguests of having a good time. You needn't worry about me. I can take care of myself."

Brandy studied him a moment, unable to hide her tiny grin. "I don't know how you do it," she remarked. "How do you stay so disciplined throughout all this?"

Raven poured a shot of Tequila while briefly eyeing her. "That's my little secret," he announced, downed the shot, and then offered a tiny hint of a smile. "If you'll excuse me, dinner will be ready in an hour."

As Raven crossed the room for the main entrance, Brandy turned on her chair and watched him until he was gone. For a servant, he had an oddly commanding presence, and Brandy was left drowning in his sex appeal. She immediately shamed herself for having the same thoughts she had scolded her friends for. The only difference was that she didn't say her thoughts aloud.

Chapter 13

Eva and Paula stared at the spotless ceiling in the library near the rolling ladder before exchanging looks, deducing that Brandy was, in fact, insane. Paula looked away, hiding her humored smile, while Eva eyed Brandy.

"I don't know what you think you saw," Eva announced, "but there's nothing there now."

"I know that, but there was blood on the ceiling, I swear," Brandy informed them, then gently rubbed her chilled shoulders. Somehow, she needed another drink. "Jana claims the house is haunted."

"Haunted?" Eva remarked while snorting a laugh. "Look around. Of course, this house is haunted!"

"I'm being serious," Brandy announced.

"So am I," Eva responded with a chuckle. "Your father was either really cool or completely fucked up."

"I'm going with the latter," Brandy muttered, then resumed with the tale of her twenty-four-hour tour of hell. "I'm seeing blood on the ceiling, and I've heard a woman screaming on two separate occasions. I'm starting to think I'm going crazy."

"Probably," Eva replied with a disinterested shrug. "Just the start of some psychotic episode, I'm sure. Knew it would happen to you sooner or later. Comes from lack of sex." Her eyes suddenly lit up. "Speaking of sex. Where's Raven? My drink needs freshening."

Brandy looked at Eva's full glass and then glared at her. "Stop it."

"I'm only teasing," Eva insisted. "Let's explore the place. I want to see these ghosts."

"I wouldn't mind a tour of the house," Paula announced, agreeing.

"Well, we have less than an hour before dinner is ready," Brandy informed her friends. "The last thing I want to do is be late." She grimaced slightly. "Raven's only been here a few hours, and he already has me whipped."

"You mean 'dominated'," Eva announced while suggestively raising her brows. "I wouldn't doubt he trades in his feather duster for a leather whip at the stroke of midnight." She groaned softly. "You lucky girl."

"I wish you'd stop sexualizing the butler," Brandy huffed.

"Come on, Brandy," Eva remarked, eyeing her. "Tell me you haven't entertained a naughty thought or two about Raven already."

Brandy hesitated, wanting to refute that claim, but Eva immediately picked up on her lack of a rapid response and laughed.

"That's what I thought."

Brandy hid her smile and blushed. "Stop it," she groaned. "Let's check out the finished basement. Attorney Rockwell said it had a wine cellar and a cigar lounge."

"Sounds promising," Paula remarked.

§

When Brandy finally found the door to the finished basement, beyond it was a curved slate staircase that descended into the long basement corridor. Despite the length of the hallway, there were only five doorways. The first door on the right was clear glass, leading into the wine cellar. The wine cellar had stone walls, a slate floor, and rows of wine shelves along three of the four walls, each containing hundreds of bottles. An elegant pub table with four chairs was set up in the middle of the room. Beyond the fourth wall was a series of three stone steps leading into a smaller wine room, which was the 'rare' room. It contained at least one hundred rare, expensive, and collectible bottles. Back in the corridor, the first door to the left was the home gym, which was massive by any standards. The gym had the same stone walls, but the floor was finished hardwood with individual mats beneath each piece of exercise equipment.

A variety of exercise equipment was present. There was a weight machine capable of any sort of weight lifting, from legs to arms; an exercise bike; a treadmill; a ski machine; a step climber; and a rower. A wall-mounted television could be rotated to any viewing angle, allowing it to be viewed from any of the equipment. In the back corner of the room, there was a steam sauna with two stone walls and one wooden wall, while the front was encased entirely in glass. Within the sauna, a long bench ran along all three walls, and the elevated pit of stones was in the center. Back in the corridor, the second door on the right was the basement powder room. The third and last door on the right was the cigar lounge. Brandy had never even heard of such a thing in a private residence before. The cigar lounge was an elegant room with hardwood floors and carved bookshelves along the back wall, which held dozens of humidors filled with cigars from around the world. The ceiling was also sculpted from wood, with soft, built-in lights, making the room just bright enough without being too bright.

There was a set of tall, leather wingback chairs, with a small table between them on both sides of the room, creating an intimate setting. It was possibly a room of 'reflection'. A meditation room of sorts for the 'refined' cigar-smoking man. There weren't any televisions or other distractions, so that must have been the idea behind the room. The second and last door on the left was the home theater. The massive room resembled a smaller movie theater with stadium seating, but with sets of plush, oversized reclining chairs. There were three rows of five, and the area in front of the wall-sized screen had two plush, round daybeds. In the back was a small bar with four pub chairs and a vintage popcorn machine. Naturally, the floor was carpeted, and the ceiling was vaulted with a small chandelier in the center. There were smaller dimmer lights along the wall, tiny lights around the stage beneath the screen, and red velvet curtains that were possibly ornamental. All three walked down the tiered rows toward the home theater's stage and screen, awestruck.

"This is awesome," Paula announced while casting herself onto one of the massive lounge chairs in front of the large viewing screen. "We're definitely watching a movie later tonight."

"We didn't find any ghosts," Eva pouted, then became excited. "We should check the unfinished basement. That'd be the perfect place to find the living challenged. There are always ghosts in basements."

"Or dead things," Paula muttered. "Let's not."

"I'm with Paula," Brandy remarked. "I haven't been in the unfinished basement yet, and I doubt I want to go down there."

"Wimp," Eva scoffed, then turned enthusiastic. "You know Randall will want to check out the basement. When are they arriving anyway?"

"Randall and Clair aren't coming until tomorrow," Brandy informed her before turning concerned. "I wish I knew where Jill was."

"I wouldn't worry about Jill," Paula remarked. "She's either an hour early or a day late."

Brandy glanced at her watch. "Dinner should be ready," she announced.

"Yes, let's not keep Raven waiting," Eva announced a little too cheerfully.

§

Later that evening, after dinner in the small, informal dining room and a movie in the home theater, the three women camped out in the game room. Paula lounged in the hot tub in her matching bra and panties while watching Eva and Brandy attempting to dance to forties swing music playing on the old-fashioned jukebox. All three women were clearly drunk and having a great time. When Brandy lost her balance and fell against the pool table, they all laughed.

"This place is great," Paula announced, then groaned while enjoying the hot tub. "When can I move in?"

"We still haven't seen any ghosts," Eva pouted. "Where are they?"

"I told you, I didn't actually see any ghosts, but there is a really creepy statue in the garden," Brandy informed them. "I swear, it vanished last night, but it was back again this morning."

"That big horse statue?" Eva asked, now intrigued. "No one could move that thing. It's made of marble, isn't it?"

"It wasn't *moved*," Brandy insisted, becoming louder. "It *vanished*."

"That maid really has you spooked," Paula retorted.

"Jana has nothing to do with it," Brandy insisted. "I know what I've seen and heard." She became increasingly agitated, although that may have had something to do with too much alcohol. "Why don't you guys believe me?"

"Well, there was that time you thought you were a panther," Paula reminded her. "That's when we knew you were going psycho."

Brandy glared at them, lacking humor. "If I remember correctly, I was deathly sick with a high fever," she reminded them. "This is completely different."

"Let's have another look at that statue," Eva announced. "Now that we're good and drunk, maybe it'll disappear for us."

"Count me out," Paula muttered and shut her eyes while sinking deeper into the hot tub with a soft, contented sigh. "I'll stay right here and allow Raven to wait on me hand and foot."

"Save some of him for me," Eva announced with a chuckle.

Chapter 14

Eva and Brandy, both clearly drunk, staggered into the garden past the fountain while laughing at nothing in particular. They finally reached the life-sized horse statue and paused before it, studying it for a moment.

"Doesn't look possessed," Eva remarked, clearly mocking her friend.

"It wasn't possessed," Brandy huffed, becoming frustrated. "It vanished."

"Well, it hasn't gone anywhere tonight," Eva remarked, almost humored, then suddenly grinned. "I wanna go for a ride."

"What?" Brandy asked, now confused by the comment.

Eva climbed up the small pedestal, then heaved herself onto the marble horse with some effort. It took two tries, and she nearly toppled off the other side. She finally found her balance and rocked on the horse's back.

"Yee ha!" Eva cried out, then looked at Brandy and laughed drunkenly. "Climb aboard. We're taking Dexter to the train station."

While Eva laughed, clearly amused, Brandy made several attempts to climb onto the statue behind her friend. When she finally made it onto the horse, Brandy almost instantly regretted sitting on the cold marble, especially in shorts. Despite the coldness, Brandy couldn't deny that it was an incredible view of the garden. Realizing she actually owned the entire estate finally set in, and, all eeriness aside, she felt unusually contented. Light from the back patio was disrupted, and a shadow appeared near them. Both looked back toward the house and saw Raven standing a couple of feet away with his hands in his pockets. Although it was not his job to judge his employer or her guests, he seemed to frown with disapproval at their behavior.

"Hey, Raven," Eva called out while kicking the statue horse in the flanks. "Help us get this damned thing started!"

"Dare I ask?" Raven muttered.

Eva laughed, finding humor in his disapproving stare, and almost slipped off. Raven approached and extended his hands to her.

"I think you've ridden enough for one night, Ms. Jericho," Raven informed her.

Eva was quick to jump into his arms as he helped her from the statue. Unfortunately for Raven, she didn't release him when she touched the ground; instead, her arms immediately circled his neck. Brandy moved up on the statue's back, closer to the withers and neck, and stared into the dark garden for a long moment despite hearing Eva drunkenly flirting with Raven.

"Is it true what they say about Englishmen?" Eva asked.

Brandy's eyes shifted to the fountain as something rippled in the water. Although she wasn't sure what she'd seen, it alarmed her. As Brandy instinctively clutched the marble horse's mane, she felt the earth move and nearly lost her balance on the statue. She uncertainly looked at the horse's stone mane with bewilderment, then leaned forward and placed her left hand on the stone neck. Raven wasn't paying attention to her since he seemed to have his hands full while attempting to remove Eva's arms from his neck. Brandy gently ran her hand along the statue's neck. To her surprise and possible horror, she felt a faint heartbeat! Brandy kept her hand on the stone neck while leaning further forward and looking at the horse's tucked, arched head. The stone eye was glowing green while turned back, looking at her. Brandy suddenly gasped and shot upright, nearly losing her balance from the quick action. When she was grabbed around the waist, she let out a startled scream before realizing it was Raven attempting to coax her off the statue.

"Come on, madam," Raven announced while gently tugging on her. "You can ride more tomorrow."

Eva stumbled closer to the fountain while singing and dancing. Brandy wasn't even paying attention to her wandering friend and barely acknowledged Raven while looking back at the statue's eyes. Brandy suddenly grabbed Raven's hand from her side and placed it on the horse's neck.

"Do you feel that?" Brandy asked.

"Yes, it's marble, and it's cold," Raven replied somewhat dryly.

Eva suddenly screamed, startling both. Brandy and Raven looked at the fountain and saw Eva laughing as she splashed and danced in the water. Raven groaned and hurried along the garden path to the fountain. Brandy laughed at her friend, then affectionately stroked the statue's neck.

"You heard Raven," Brandy informed the horse. "We can ride more tomorrow."

Brandy heard another scream and looked up in time to witness Eva pulling Raven into the fountain with her. Both crashed into the water with a massive splash. When she surfaced, Eva laughed uncontrollably. Brandy suddenly heard a loud crumbling sound followed by a thump as the statue shifted. She cried out as she lost her balance and toppled off the horse, missing the statue base and hitting the soft ground. Brandy groaned softly as she pulled herself to her hands and knees and looked at the statue. The horse's once raised hoof was now planted firmly on the foundation.

Chapter 15

Within the master bedroom, Brandy sat on the bench at the foot end of her bed and held a cloth to the cut on her temple while Raven, now changed into dry, more casual clothes, partially kneeled before her and cleaned the scrape on her shin. Despite the lingering effects of the alcohol and her throbbing head, she was consciously aware of her foot propped on Raven's knee and his free hand holding her bare calf while he doctored her injury. Brandy watched him attentively and delicately tend to her bleeding leg. The action was unintentionally intimate, but she was also painfully aware that Raven's first day working for her would probably be his last, and she couldn't blame him. Neither she nor her friends made a very good first impression on him. She sluggishly pulled the cloth back from her temple and looked at the small amount of blood.

"Did the bleeding stop?" Raven asked while applying two larger Band-Aids to her shin wound.

Brandy nodded, immediately regretting the action, and then groaned. "Talk about a sobering experience," she muttered.

Raven sighed and moved onto the bench seat alongside her to examine her head wound. As he gently brushed the hair from her temple, she met his gaze. His eyes only briefly met hers, which was a bad sign, and he looked over the cut and bruise.

"You should really see a doctor," Raven insisted. "I could drive you--"

"I'm fine. I'm not going to the hospital," Brandy informed him somewhat abruptly, then frowned. "It's too embarrassing."

"In your defense," he announced, "stupidity is a common side effect of alcohol."

Brandy couldn't take her eyes off him despite his inability to look at her. She screwed up, and he was quitting in the morning. All she could do was offer a heartfelt apology and hope for the best.

"I didn't make a very good impression on you, did I?" Brandy muttered, working her way up to her apology.

"It doesn't really matter what I think," Raven replied while gently cleaning the cut. "I'm paid to kiss your ass."

Brandy maintained her stare, somewhat surprised by the remark. Was it possible he wasn't even bothered by her drunken antics?

"Do I pay extra for the sarcasm?" she asked, unable to stop the words before they left her mouth.

Another side effect of alcohol. No filter between her brain and her mouth.

"Actually, I offer that service for free," Raven casually replied, then briefly met her gaze and raised his brows. "But I do charge extra for my medical services."

Brandy eyed him somewhat suspiciously, not sure if he was being serious or sarcastic. Perhaps there was little danger of his quitting after all.

"Do you come with instructions or must I buy a whip?" Brandy remarked.

As he finished taping small strips across the cut on her temple, a smile crossed his face before his serious demeanor returned.

"You should get some rest," Raven informed her as he finished dressing her injury. "I'll check on you throughout the night and make sure you don't have a concussion."

As Raven stood, gathering the discarded medical supplies, Brandy weighed his words and gauged his intentions.

"I suppose you'll be handing in your resignation in the morning," Brandy remarked, then frowned. "Hasn't exactly been a great first day working for me. Especially after what happened with Eva and the fountain." She groaned, defeated. "I'm a lousy employer."

"Perhaps, but I'm a lousy butler," Raven replied. "So it's a good fit." Raven then smirked and added a low chuckle. "Don't worry about it. I can handle you and your friends."

Brandy studied him a moment before cocking her head, not quite understanding. "You can *handle* us?" she asked. "What's that supposed to mean?"

Raven smirked, hiding his amusement. "Buy a whip."

Raven's mannerisms and the words spoken sent a slight tingly sensation throughout her body. As Raven left the room, shutting the door behind him, Brandy stared after him, still pondering his words. She suddenly grinned and held back her laugh. Whether he was being cute, perverted, or facetious, it didn't matter. Raven was a keeper. Once Raven was gone, Brandy changed for bed and crawled under the covers of the massive, king-sized bed. She was drunk and exhausted. The world spun for a few minutes before she slipped into a deep sleep. Despite her particularly horrifying nightmares, Raven seemed to be in every dream, derailing the nightmares and bringing peace to her sleep.

§

When Brandy woke the following morning to the sun poking through the part in the curtains, she realized she'd survived the night without feeling the need to lock herself in the bathroom. Somewhat disturbing was the sexually explicit dream she'd had with Raven just before waking up. Brandy was slightly ashamed while feeling sexually charged. With the way she felt, if Raven had been in the room with her at that moment, she would have happily played out some of her naughtier dreams for him. After entertaining a fantasy or two with the handsome butler, she was reminded of her aching head, and the scene in the garden suddenly came flooding back to her. It took her a moment or two to piece together what she remembered, and she was instantly alarmed.

Chapter 16

Late morning. Eva's guestroom may have been smaller than the master bedroom, but it was definitely brighter and lighter. The walls had light burgundy wallpaper, curtains, and a matching bedspread. There was a small sitting area that included a light-colored fainting couch, a chair, and a footrest. The king-sized bed had a tall, hardtop canopy in light walnut, with four thick, round bedposts, while two light colored throw rugs helped brighten the hardwood floor. The shower was heard running in the bathroom beyond the closed door. Steam partially filled the bathroom as Eva stood within the massive standing shower beneath the hot streams of water from several showerheads, all blasting at once. Eva's bathroom was lavishly appointed with a sunken garden tub encased in tile in front of two large windows for a fantastic view. A built-in decorative bookcase of sorts was placed as a partition to section off the double-wide standing shower made from the same tan and brown tile as the tub casing and floor.

The shower was made of clear, solid glass with multiple jetted showerheads, located not far from the elaborate dressing table. The toilet was beyond its own door, keeping it separate from the two bathing areas. Expensive curtains and a set of crystal chandeliers gave the already ritzy bathroom an even wealthier appearance. Eva appeared half asleep while undeniably enjoying the hot streams of water striking her from several directions. She moaned while holding onto the wall in front and alongside her for added support, her forehead resting against the wall, and her eyes remaining closed. Water surrounding the drain gurgled and slurped as she remained oblivious to the sound. Decaying flesh-covered fingers rose from the drain. Eva's eyes remained closed, and she still didn't move from her comfortable spot in the shower. As she moaned again and shifted under the water, the rotting hand and arm now emerged from the drain as well. The hand felt around the shower floor, only inches from her feet, and was getting closer. Suddenly, there was an urgent pounding on the bathroom door. Eva gasped with alarm and opened her eyes.

"Eva, I need to talk to you," Brandy called through the door. "It's important!"

Before she even saw it, the decayed hand disappeared back down the drain. Eva groaned while grabbing the towel hanging over the glass shower wall, wrapped it around herself, and stepped out. She wearily traipsed across the massive bathroom to the door and opened it, glaring at her friend, not humored. Brandy stood in the doorway with a frazzled, concerned look on her face.

"You have to come with me!" Brandy announced urgently.

"Does it require clothes?" Eva moaned.

"This is important," Brandy insisted. "Hurry! Get dressed. I have something to show you. I'll get Paula and meet you in the garden."

As Brandy disappeared from the doorway, Eva rolled her eyes with a low groan.

"I wish, just once, she was the one with a hangover," Eva muttered.

§

Brandy, Eva, and Paula stood in the garden around the horse statue, staring at it. Eva was less than impressed, while Paula appeared disgusted and possibly annoyed.

"You're insane, Brandy," Paula scoffed. "You were drunk last night. We all were."

"Speak for yourself," Eva muttered despite being clearly hungover.

"I wouldn't make it up, and I wasn't having a drunken hallucination," Brandy insisted, becoming frustrated. "The statue moved, and that's why I fell off." She touched the statue's neck, hesitated, and then eyed her friends. "You can feel it. There's something inside."

"You're losing it," Paula huffed while folding her arms across her chest.

Eva played along, touched the statue, then shook her head. "I don't feel anything," she insisted. "It's just a large piece of marble, Brandy."

"Planning another ride?" Raven asked from behind them.

All three jumped with surprise and spun toward the house, where Raven stood only a few feet from them, eyeing them almost suspiciously.

"I didn't mean to startle you," Raven announced, although that had clearly been his intention with the way he seemed to move around in stealth mode.

Brandy could barely look at Raven after the graphic sexual dreams she had with him. The level of intensity was enough to make her blush just being a few feet away from him.

"I was just wondering what you'd like for brunch today," Raven remarked. "I recommend Thorazine sautéed in a mild anti-psychotic sauce."

Eva glared at Brandy, humorless and hungover. "Can we have him fixed?" she muttered.

"For your next birthday," Brandy replied.

Raven eyed Brandy and smirked. She knew it was because he heard their conversation, but she still felt as if he knew about her sexual dreams involving him. Brandy immediately fidgeted while hiding her tell-tale grin.

"How's your head?" Raven asked, eyeing her.

Brandy immediately tensed at the question, then realized he'd meant her head injury from last night. She really needed to scrub those dreams from her mind. Brandy gingerly touched the carefully taped wound on her temple.

"I have a dull, lingering headache," Brandy informed him. "But my embarrassment is worse than the pain."

"I'd like to change the dressing and take a look at the cut," Raven remarked. "I can probably help with your headaches as well."

"I'd appreciate that," Brandy remarked, then chuckled softly. "Add it to my bill."

§

After brunch, Eva and Paula changed into their swimsuits and enjoyed the warm afternoon in the pool and the outdoor hot tub while Brandy stayed behind in the kitchen so Raven could change the dressing on her head laceration. Since she also had abrasions on her leg, there would be no pool or hot tub for her anyway. Brandy sat on one of the island counter stools, elevating her so Raven didn't have to hunch over while tending to her injury. Brandy couldn't deny she wasn't exactly sitting on the tall pub chair in the most ladylike fashion, practically manspreading. Still, when Raven stood before her between her legs, she had to wonder if it was purposeful or just coincidental. The action made Brandy tense only because of her early morning erotic dreams involving Raven. While Jana cleaned up from brunch, she cast odd, possibly scornful looks at Raven. Brandy pretended she didn't see the way Jana glared, but it was making her uncomfortable. It put a serious damper on the unintentional erotic moment she was attempting to savor. While gently cleaning the wound around the steri-strips, Raven cast a quick look at her.

"I'm not hurting you, am I?" he asked.

"No," Brandy replied, then gently cleared her throat before speaking softly. "What's with the death glares from Jana?"

"Want me to ask?" he replied in the same soft tone, possibly mocking her.

Brandy chuckled softly. "No, that's quite all right," she replied.

Raven hesitated, then reached for the antibiotic ointment while casting a look at Jana. "Why don't you take your break, Jana?" he announced. "I can take care of the rest."

Jana eyed him, then Brandy, before nodding. She left the room, heading into the staff wing without comment. Raven looked back at Brandy, his face close to hers.

"Better?"

Brandy could almost feel the color rising to her cheeks. Now, she only had to worry about her own behavior. Once he applied the dressing, Brandy was grateful that she had survived without throwing herself at the butler. The temptation had been very strong, and he wasn't making it any easier on her. Without moving from his position between her knees, he eyed her while cocking his head.

"Do you still have a headache?"

"Yes," she replied while frowning. "Although it's not a migraine yet."

"I have a cure for that," Raven informed her. "It's unconventional, but you can trust me."

Brandy eyed him almost suspiciously. "An ex-boyfriend said the same thing once," she remarked.

Raven attempted to hide his smirk, somehow knowing the 'code'. "Did it work?" he asked.

Brandy had to consider it. "Actually, it did," she replied, then snorted a laugh.

Raven chuckled and avoided looking at her. "My cure is a little less 'familiar'," he teased. "We can both keep our clothes on."

Brandy couldn't even look him in the eyes as the color rushed to her cheeks. "I'm willing to put a little trust in you," she replied while watching him with anticipation.

Raven placed his index and middle fingers from each hand on her temples, just above her ears, applying light pressure while gently massaging. Brandy shut her eyes, unable to deny that it felt good, although she was kind of nostalgic for the 'other' method. After a minute or two, he pulled away. Brandy opened her eyes, glanced at him, and seemed to consider what had just happened.

"Huh," she announced, then grinned. "That actually worked." Brandy then laughed. "Do you know any other tricks?"

"I have more than a few tricks up my sleeve," Raven remarked with a sly grin.

"Maybe you'll show me a few more sometime," Brandy announced.

"I'm sure I will."

Brandy felt an erotic shockwave shoot through her entire body at his words, mixed with his tone and sexy accent. She avoided looking at him, knowing her cheeks were flushed, and gently bit her lower lip to keep from adding more fuel to her already burning fire of desire. Raven gently cleared his throat as he moved away from her.

"I should get back to work," he announced.

And just when she was starting to have fun. Brandy easily hid her disappointment and took her cue. It was for the best.

Chapter 17

Eva sat in the sunroom at the back of the mansion just off the terrace, paging through an old book. She glanced outside, appeared curious, and then lowered the book with a low groan. Brandy and Paula were seen searching the area surrounding the statue while Raven casually leaned against it, his hands in his pockets, and watched them. There was a good chance he thought Brandy was crazy. Eva continued staring out the window, almost ashamed of her friends, when she heard a faint voice from beyond both sets of interior doors. She looked across the room, now curious, set her book aside, and quietly approached the first set of doors. The voice appeared louder now, but the hall was empty. Eva entered the hallway, following the faint female voice, and paused outside the partially open door to the formal dining room. She could clearly hear Jana talking to someone. Considering Raven was in the garden with her crazy friends, she had to wonder who Jana was speaking with.

"I'll need some time to think about that," Jana announced, although no one else was heard responding.

Eva stepped into the dining room doorway and casually looked around. Keeping in theme with the entire gothic tone the rest of the mansion had set, the formal dining room didn't disappoint. The bold wallpaper was a deep, vibrant red with a slightly bluish hue. The floor-to-ceiling stained-glass windows covered a vast portion of the outer wall, with fifteen-foot-tall red curtains held back by red and black satin sashes. Two massive, moderately creepy chandeliers dangled from thick chains above the long, heavy, dark table, which had an almost medieval appearance. The twelve chairs were tall and pointy with red velvet seats that matched the long, velvet tablecloth. A crimson, black, and gray throw carpet covered the highly glossed hardwood floor beneath the table and chairs. In addition to the table, there was a large, decorative sideboard along the inner wall and a small bar near the kitchen entrance.

On the far wall was another massive, black marble fireplace with a large, framed medieval painting above it. As an added security measure, a suit of armor stood guard on either side of the main entrance. Eva's eyes then fell upon Jana, who was arranging the tableware with her back to the doorway, unaware of Eva's presence.

"Nothing's ever as simple as you think," Jana remarked, matter-of-factly.

Eva again glanced around the clearly empty room. When Jana turned and saw her, she let out a startled gasp, surprised by her presence.

"You startled me," Jana announced, then managed a tiny smile.

Eva again scanned the room with a puzzled look before meeting Jana's gaze. "Who were you talking to?" she asked.

"Uh, well," Jana remarked while fidgeting. "The ghosts." She then looked around and grimaced. "I think you've frightened them."

Eva stared at her a moment longer with a look of disbelief, then attempted a tiny smile. "Uh, huh," she remarked. "Okay, well, if you see them again, you should introduce me. I've been looking everywhere for those guys."

Eva offered a tense smile, leaving Jana slightly dumbfounded by the comment, and then returned to the hallway. She shook her head with a tiny, humored chuckle just before Brandy and Paula appeared from the kitchen. Eva was now amused as she approached them.

"I'm afraid you've just missed the spooks and specters," Eva announced.

"What?" Brandy asked, dumbfounded.

"Jana was just holding a conversation with one of them," Eva remarked while indicating the dining room. "That's one strange girl you have there."

"Obviously, your father didn't hire her for her winning personality," Paula remarked.

"I'm doubting he hired her for her work performance either," Brandy muttered.

"With a body like that, a woman doesn't need a personality or excellent work ethics, if you know what I mean," Paula replied while suggestively raising her brows.

Brandy rolled her eyes and groaned. "Let's not go there," she muttered. "I don't want to think about my father 'doing' the young maid."

"You're the one who always said he was probably some Playboy bastard," Eva reminded her.

"I know, but that doesn't mean I want to find out it's true," Brandy remarked.

§

Within the game room later that afternoon, Brandy sat at the small pub table, sipping iced tea, while watching Eva and Paula play a game of pool. The trash talk was flying as the two, both highly competitive women, tried to break a tie. Jana entered the game room, looking perkier than she had since Raven's arrival, and approached Brandy.

"I'm sorry to disturb you, Ms. Holloway," Jana announced. "I can't find Raven. He went to the wine cellar to find a bottle for dinner, but he seems to have disappeared. He's been gone almost an hour and didn't leave any further instructions for me regarding this afternoon."

"Oh," Brandy announced and stood, receiving looks from her friends between plays. "I'll find him." She then hesitated and looked at Jana. "Where's the wine cellar again?"

"Alongside the cigar lounge in the basement," Jana replied. "Near the gym and the theater."

Brandy smiled with some embarrassment. "I'll eventually find my way around here," she remarked.

As Jana headed back for the kitchen, Brandy headed for the door to the finished basement. She opened the door and found it was a closet. The door she saw next was the one that would take her to the wine cellar. It seemed odd that Raven would just vanish on Jana like that. He was well aware of her inability to self-motivate. When she reached the bottom of the stairs, Brandy hesitated. She smelled cigar smoke, but she wasn't sure why. Rather than head into the wine cellar, Brandy entered the cigar lounge. She paused in the doorway when she saw Raven comfortably seated in one of the old leather chairs, puffing on a cigar with a glass of whiskey on the small table near him. He appeared to be off in his own world, a solemn expression on his face. Brandy stood in the doorway a moment longer, watching the regal manner in which Raven smoked the cigar. It would be impossible for him to look any sexier. When Brandy lightly tapped on the open door, Raven turned his head, saw her, and sprang up from the chair.

"I'm terribly sorry, madam," he announced and quickly turned to crush his cigar.

"No, as you were," Brandy replied, not really sure what the proper terms were, but went with military jargon.

Raven remained slightly tense, seemingly struggling to decide if he'd return to 'as he was' or if he'd resume his duties.

"I'd given Jana enough chores to keep her busy for an hour or so," he informed her. "I, uh, figured it was a good time to take a break."

Brandy approached and collapsed into the chair opposite the small table. "And you should take more breaks," she insisted. "You rarely stop working."

As she indicated for him to sit back down, Brandy wondered if Jana purposely sent her into the wine cellar so she'd catch Raven drinking and smoking. Raven hesitated a moment, pondering his options, and then returned to the seat.

"I, uh, like this room," he informed her while gesturing with his cigar in hand. "I find it *calming*."

"Anyone in particular have you stressed?" Brandy asked, curious.

"If you're referring to Jana, I'm used to being hated by the staff," Raven replied, then uncertainly puffed on the cigar.

Brandy felt compelled to watch him, unable to hide her tiny smile. "My mother's boyfriend," she began, then hesitated. "My mother's *ex-boyfriend* would smoke cigars on the terrace at her house. When he was having a glass of libation and a cigar, he'd open up about all sorts of things." Brandy managed a tiny chuckle. "My mother said it was better than pillow talk."

"Scotch has a way of loosening the tongue," Raven remarked with a soft chuckle.

"Yeah, he was a scotch man too," she announced, then hesitated and picked up his glass, sniffing it. "Though this smells like whiskey."

"The bottle was open and nearly empty," Raven informed her. "I hope you don't mind."

"Of course not," Brandy insisted. "It's going to be a long weekend for you. Do whatever you need to do to cope. I don't want you quitting on me."

"You're safe," he insisted with a tiny smile. "Although I believe you need my medical services more than my domestic ones."

Brandy had to smile at the comment. "You've kind of caught me at my worst," she informed him. "I've made better first, second, and third impressions." She rubbed her chilled arms and shivered, even though it wasn't cold. "It's this place."

Raven placed his cigar on the ashtray, stood, and swiftly removed his jacket. Without a moment's hesitation, he put it over her shoulders, then returned to his chair and his cigar. Brandy enjoyed the musky scent of his aftershave mixed with the smoky, expensive cigar. She glanced at his profile as he puffed on the cigar, drawing it out, as if taking his last breath.

"I'm glad you're here, Raven," she announced almost too softly for him to hear.

Raven looked at her, possibly surprised by the admission, and smiled. "I'm glad you tolerate me," he replied.

"*I* tolerate *you*?" she asked, then snorted a laugh. "That's a good one. I'm not one for being pampered. I'm a working girl. I don't want to be anyone's boss."

"I've been told I'm 'difficult', and 'I don't play well with others'," Raven informed her. "I kind of like to do my own thing. Not exactly 'proper butler etiquette'."

"Then I guess you're a good fit here," Brandy informed him.

"Did I mention 'snarky' and 'arrogant'?"

Brandy eyed him and met his gaze. She had to laugh. "Yeah, I already figured that out," she remarked.

Raven put out his cigar and then picked up the glass of whiskey. "Drinks on the job, too," he announced, then drank the entire contents in one swallow before standing. "Back to the wine selection for tonight."

Brandy jumped to her feet, removed his jacket from her shoulders, then handed it to him. Once Raven slipped into his jacket, Brandy felt the need to smooth the lapels for him. When she lifted her eyes, she realized he was staring down at her. She smiled and walked away.

Chapter 18

Late afternoon. Brandy stood behind the bar in the game room, fixing drinks for her friends a couple of hours before dinner, when Raven entered with a man and a woman following. They were Brandy's friends, Randall and Clair. Randall was a suave, handsome man in his mid-to-late twenties. Standing roughly six feet tall, he had an athletic build and a regal stance. His dark hair was moderately short and meticulously styled, while his longer sideburns went down into what he referred to as a light beard, although it technically looked like a dark, five o'clock shadow. Randall had the looks, style, and sophistication of a runway model. He was work-driven, which was both his greatest attribute and his biggest downfall. Clair, a blonde bombshell with pale blue eyes, was in her early to mid-twenties. She was relatively short and had a lean build. Her straight blonde hair hung down beyond her shoulders and just about touched her ample cleavage. She was as sexy as she was business-oriented, making her and Randall a great match.

Paula and Eva squealed and ran to their friends, hugging them before Raven had a chance to introduce them formally. By the time Brandy made it out from behind the bar and joined them, they were finished hugging Paula and Eva. Both greeted Brandy with enthusiasm and looked around the game room.

"This place is amazing," Clair announced, delighted.

"You never mentioned that your father was rich," Randall remarked.

Brandy shrugged, almost uninterested. "Well, considering I didn't know him, I wouldn't have known if he had been wealthy."

"We definitely want the grand tour," Clair announced.

"Where's Jill?" Randall asked, then appeared curious. "She didn't get drunk and pass out already, I hope."

"We were wondering where she was as well," Paula remarked. "You'd think she'd call if she couldn't make it."

Randall was suddenly confused. "What do you mean?" he asked. "Wasn't that her maroon sports car I saw parked in front of the garage?"

Brandy stared at Randall a moment, sharing his confusion, then looked at Raven. "Would you mind checking on that?"

"Yes, madam," Raven replied, then left the game room.

"Check out that bar," Randall announced while approaching it, then looked back at Brandy. "Mind if I help myself?"

"Go right ahead," Brandy replied. "I know you like playing bartender."

"Bartending got me through college," Randall reminded her while grinning. "I was pretty good at it."

"Make a pitcher of your famous green tea shots," Clair insisted. "Randall and I need to get our buzz on if we want to catch up to you three."

"Only one for me," Brandy announced with a soft groan. "I had too much to drink last night and made an ass of myself." She then indicated the small piece of medical tape on her temple. "I'm not going there again tonight."

"I made an ass of myself last night, too," Eva informed her. "But I'm still getting my buzz on tonight. You're a lightweight."

"Drink as much as you want," Brandy informed her friend. "Just keep your hands off Raven."

"Oh?" Clair asked while slyly looking at her friends. "The three of you already fighting over the handsome butler?" She groaned and shook her head. "The moment I heard that accent, I knew the claws would be coming out over him."

"No, we're not fighting over Raven," Brandy insisted, then indicated Eva. "Eva was just testing the boundaries of sexual harassment. Thankfully, Raven is a good sport."

"I'll behave myself tonight, I promise," Eva insisted, then snorted a laugh while grinning. "But the memories will last a lifetime."

Once Randall made a pitcher of green tea shots, he poured a round for everyone, and the five toasted to Brandy's new house and good fortune. They drank the flavorful shot and returned their glasses to the bar. Randall poured another round for everyone except Brandy, then briefly eyed her.

"So how about that tour?" Randall asked.

"We can start by showing you to your room," Brandy informed him. "But we'll wait for Raven to return. I have no idea which bedroom he had Jana freshen for you."

"What's the deal with your new butler?" Clair finally asked, eyeing her three female friends. "Is he single?"

"Standing right here," Randall informed her before downing his second shot.

"I wasn't asking for me, dear," Clair scoffed, then looked back at her friends. "Handsome guy like that, British no less. Surely one of you has your eyes on him."

"Honestly," Eva announced. "He thinks we're all a little crazy."

"Speak for yourself," Paula remarked. "I'm not the one seeing and hearing things."

"We're saving him for Brandy," Eva insisted and downed her second shot. "Her house; her butler. She gets first shot."

"You're awful," Brandy scolded her friend.

"Oh, come on," Eva groaned. "You know you want him. I've seen the way you look at him."

Randall poured another round for the four of them, excluding Brandy once again. Brandy considered Eva's comment and managed a tiny shrug.

"He's undeniably handsome," Brandy replied. "And if I had a type, I'm pretty sure he'd be it." She managed a tiny laugh. "Another good reason to stay sober. I don't want to say or do something that'll make him uncomfortable."

"My God, Brandy," Paula finally groaned. "Just admit you want him and get on with it."

"I'm not admitting anything," Brandy insisted while hiding her grin. "I plead the fifth."

"Pardon me, madam," Raven announced only a few feet from behind Brandy, startling her.

Brandy spun, surprised to see Raven standing behind her as if he hadn't heard any of their inappropriate conversation. Brandy placed her hand to her chest and groaned softly.

"I wish you wouldn't sneak up on me like that," Brandy gasped.

"I wasn't aware that I was sneaking," Raven casually replied. "If you'd like, I could announce myself when I enter the room."

Brandy stared at Raven, who stared back. Although his expression never changed, she wasn't sure if he was being serious or not.

"That's not necessary," Brandy replied while fidgeting with embarrassment over what he'd possibly heard.

"There are several cars by the garage," Raven informed her. "None were maroon, and I didn't see anyone outside."

"What about the workshop alongside the garage?" Brandy asked.

"The workshop was locked," Raven replied.

Brandy glanced at her friends while fidgeting. "I'm going to have a look around outside by the garage and the workshop," she informed them. "I'll be back."

"Shall I come along?" Raven asked.

Eva and Paula eyed Brandy and suggestively raised their brows, hinting for her to take him up on the offer of some one-on-one time.

"No, that's okay," Brandy replied, doing her best to ignore her friends and keep her cheeks from flushing. "Just, uh, make sure everyone's taken care of."

Chapter 19

Brandy stood outside the old gardener's workshop. Compared with the rest of the estate, it was the only thing that appeared untouched and in need of a little TLC. The rusted doorknob was locked, forcing her to try several keys in the old lock. It took several keys before she found the right one. Thankfully, the lock wasn't rusted shut. Of course, if it had been, then there would obviously be no way Jill would be in the workshop. As it was, entering the building seemed like a reach. The door was locked. How would Jill have gotten inside in the first place? Brandy slowly opened the door and looked around. The workshop was dark and more than a little creepy. She hated to admit that she was a bit spooked entering, but she stepped inside, just to be sure her friend wasn't there. Without touching anything, she approached the dusty workbench and saw four streaks disturbing the thick dust on the edge of the counter.

Brandy looked around with concern. Someone had been inside the workshop! She then saw deep scratches on the outside of the bench just near the bottom. Brandy crouched near the workbench and hesitantly looked into the dark space behind it. She was certain she saw something and reached into the opening, feeling around. There was a loud snap. Brandy cried out and jumped backward, falling onto her backside while shaking the old mousetrap from her fingers. She leapt to her feet while holding her right hand, which was now red and throbbed. She'd seen enough. Brandy spun and nearly collided with Raven. She let out a horrified scream and jumped back a step, striking the old workbench. Raven stared at her and appeared a little too calm.

"Damn it, you scared me!" Brandy cried out.

"I thought you were in trouble," Raven replied, barely reacting. He then noticed her holding her right hand. "Are you okay?"

Brandy gingerly rubbed her sore fingers. "Just a mousetrap," she informed him. "Scared me more than anything."

"Your friend, Paula, said it's her car parked in front of the garage," Raven informed her. "Though she insists she didn't park it there."

"Who would move her car?"

"I assure you I didn't," Raven replied. "But your gentleman friend insists that wasn't the car he saw when he arrived."

Brandy was now thoroughly confused while staring at Raven. "None of this makes any sense," she insisted.

"I'm sure there's a plausible explanation for everything," he assured her.

Brandy huffed and folded her arms across her chest, challenging that. "Such as--?"

"Perhaps your friends are playing some sort of elaborate prank," Raven replied, coming up with a response just a little too quickly for her liking.

"My friends aren't really the practical joker types," she informed him.

"Perhaps we should get some ice for your hand," Raven remarked, refusing to comment on her assessment of her friends. Maybe he didn't believe her.

"My hand is fine," she insisted.

Raven studied her a moment before indicating her hair. "You have a little something--" he announced, then removed something from her hair.

The action itself was a bit endearing, if not cliché. Raven opened his hand and eyed the fat, hairy spider that was nearly the size of his palm. Brandy cried out and jumped back, again striking the workbench while staring at the terrifying spider, which Raven seemed to be casually admiring. He noticed her reaction and immediately set it free on a nearby, rusted lawn tractor.

"Would you like to go back inside now?" Raven asked.

Brandy nervously ran her trembling fingers through her hair. "Yes, definitely," she insisted. "I need a drink." She then met his gaze. "And, don't take this the wrong way, but I'm going to need you to check me over for anymore spiders."

Without further comment, she hurried past him for the entrance. Raven followed her out of the workshop without question. Once they were outside, he finally spoke.

"I assume you aren't a fan of spiders, madam," he remarked.

Brandy paused outside the door and spun to face him, about to profess her discontent for the hairy beasts, when she saw Raven snatch something from her shoulder. He quickly stood at attention, placing his hands almost suspiciously behind his back. She cocked her head lightly to the side while eyeing him.

"What was that?" she demanded.

"Nothing," he casually replied.

Brandy saw him lightly flick something from his hands behind his back. She looked down and saw another fat spider flip right-side up and scurry away. She immediately met his somewhat innocent gaze regarding the spider he attempted to hide from her, and glared at him.

"I don't care where you put your hands or what you have to touch," she announced sternly. "If there are any more spiders on me, get them off now!"

§

The formal dining room table was set with crimson salad plates on top of black dinner plates, alongside medieval silverware and red crystal wine goblets. The centerpiece was mostly red carnations in a black vase with black candelabras on either side holding five red candles. The sideboard had two matching single candlesticks on either side of a smaller vase with red roses. It was their first formal dinner in the larger room, since they had eaten their other meals in the smaller one. When Brandy and her friends entered the oddly gothic-looking formal dining room, her friends were in awe, but mostly because it looked as if vampires were preparing to feast. Hearing her friends' soft comments and tiny snickers, Brandy again thought about the house and its whole creepy motif, yet Raven didn't even seem fazed by any of it. From everything she'd ever heard about proper butlers, they were supposed to be indifferent to things around them, but Brandy didn't understand *how* he could pretend any of this was normal.

They were served a surprisingly delicious meal that Raven obviously prepared, as Jana couldn't even manage simple things. Raven set the mood to match the dining room, and her friends couldn't get enough of it. Every detail, from the red candles dripping wax that looked like blood to red crystal salt and pepper shakers in the form of dragons. Dinner was an exceptionally rare roast beef, some sort of red glazed potatoes, and unusually black bread. Whatever they were eating, it tasted good. On a scale from one to ten, the creep factor at Brandy's little dinner party hit an eleven and would be something they'd talk about for years to come. When Jana and Raven served dessert, her friends were giddy at the chocolate lava cake that oozed red raspberry filling, almost resembling blood. Brandy was starting to wonder if Raven wasn't having a little too much fun elevating the disturbing atmosphere. He seemed almost too serious the entire time, yet this was the man who drank shots while on duty. Brandy desperately wanted to get inside his head and figure him out.

After screams and laughs about the cake erupting blood, Brandy and her friends finished their blood red wine while continuing their earlier conversation as Jana and Raven cleared away the dessert plates. Randall leaned back in his chair, swirled the wine in his glass, and eyed Brandy with a humored smile.

"Eva tells me you're afraid to go into the basement," Randall remarked.

"I'm not afraid to go into the basement," Brandy insisted. "I just don't want to." She sneered at the thought. "Probably crawling with spiders."

"There could be a fortune in antiques down there," Randall informed her. "We have to at least look."

"Can't you forget about work for one weekend, Randall?" Clair demanded, then turned to Brandy. "Don't let him talk you into selling anything. Our antique shop is filled to the ceiling."

"There's no reason to go into the basement," Brandy insisted. "I doubt there's anything down there that'll interest you and your warped basement obsession."

"I don't have a warped basement obsession," Randall scoffed while shifting almost uncomfortably. "I like creepy things."

"He gets off on it," Clair muttered.

"That is definitely not true," Randall huffed.

"Then explain that creepy medieval torture painting of two guys chained in a dungeon with a third on the stretching rack," Clair remarked.

"It's an antique, and it's worth thousands," Randall insisted in his defense.

"You hung it in our bedroom," Clair scoffed.

"Where did you want me to hang it?" he demanded. "In the bathroom?"

"We should check out the basement," Eva insisted, siding with Randall and practically begging Brandy. "Maybe we'll finally find some ghosts."

Clair appeared interested and looked at Eva. "Ghosts?"

"Now whose warped obsession is showing?" Randall muttered to his girlfriend.

"Brandy thinks this house is haunted," Paula informed Clair. "The horse statue bucked her off last night."

Brandy groaned and covered her eyes. "Not again," she muttered.

"Come on, Brandy," Randall begged. "We *have* to check out the basement. It's probably all dark and creepy with mutant spiders."

Clair glared at her boyfriend and shook her head. "You are *so* bizarre."

Chapter 20

*U*nlike the wine cellar stairs, the basement stairs descended two stories, making it more of a sub-basement. The first flight of stone steps seemed almost normal. Winding down to the second level, the steps became less even, as if carved from stone, etched into the earth, and the handrail seemed to have disappeared. The walls were of natural stone, with mounted wrought-iron light fixtures, and the electrical lines were tacked to the stone itself. The bottom of the stairs opened up into what could only be described as a dungeon. Still without handrails, the stairs went four feet beyond the last of the wall. One step to the side would result in a nasty fall. Randall appeared at the bottom of the basement stairs first and looked around. He suddenly stopped, smiled, and chuckled in an almost sinister manner.

"Oh, this is so creepy!"

Brandy cautiously followed Paula, Clair, and Eva down the remaining steps, keeping a close watch on the network of cobwebs. It was a spider's paradise! When she saw the stone corridor, she almost turned around. Unfortunately, Eva clung to her hand and stopped her. The dungeon corridor was almost as long as the grand hallway, although not nearly as broad; it was definitely as tall, if not taller. The walls, floor, and ceiling were made entirely of block stone, with the high ceiling arched the entire distance. Rather than rooms, the many doorways were encased in wrought iron, medieval cell doors. It was as if stepping into another century, and not a pleasant one. Although there were several electric light fixtures throughout the eerie corridor, it was also lined with oil lamps and torches. Obviously, none were lit. At the end of the corridor was a solid, thick wooden door.

Brandy rubbed her chilled arms and shivered. "Well, this is going to give me nightmares tonight," she muttered.

Eva groaned and pulled her along, deeper into what was clearly a dungeon. Randall was laughing the entire way down the broad corridor, looking into each cell, disappointed when each was empty. Brandy looked in each cell as well, fearful she'd actually see a skeleton chained to the walls. Curse her overactive imagination. Randal finally reached the solid door at the far end of the lengthy corridor. He pushed open the heavy door and peered inside. His demonic laugh increased.

"Oh! You guys are not going to believe this!" Randall cried out as he disappeared inside the room. "This is awesome."

That was all Brandy had to hear to know it was going to be bad. She reluctantly followed her friends into the room, with little choice since Eva refused to let go of her wrist. Once inside, Brandy was stunned at what she saw. It wasn't a room. It was a torture chamber! The torture chamber was something straight out of a horror movie. With the same walls, floor, and ceiling design as the corridor, the chamber itself was two or three rooms separated by broad, arched openings. There were only two electric light fixtures near the main entrance, leaving the rest of the room dimly lit, making it even creepier, if that were possible. There were several torches and oil lamps attached to the walls that also remained unlit. Along the walls were several sets of medieval shackles staked into the stone, while an array of torture devices occupied the massive spaces within each of the rooms. Among the torture devices, there was a spiked chair, an enormous Iron Maiden, and a stretching rack. There was other 'furniture' as well, but they looked more like blocks of wood with shackles attached, some with large holes in them. A rack on the nearby wall appeared to hold the 'tools of the trade'. There were iron tools of varying types, whose uses were speculative and probably deeply horrifying.

Brandy rolled her eyes and attempted to leave, but Eva pulled her back inside. The Iron Maiden was a tall sarcophagus-shaped cabinet, aptly made of iron, in the shape of a woman. The inside front doors and back wall were lined with long, sharp spikes. It was a menacing-looking piece of hardware. The mere sight of it, with its two doors standing open, was enough to instill fear in those within the torture chamber.

Randall, unwilling to let a moment to frighten the women go unpassed, announced, "The prisoner was placed inside this nasty, bad boy, and the doors were slowly closed so the spikes pierced the body in mostly non-vital areas. This way he *or she* slowly bled to death." He suddenly grinned, almost enthusiastic. "Horribly barbaric."

"Do you think these are authentic?" Clair asked while running her finger along the Iron Maiden.

"They can't be," Brandy remarked while checking out the spiked chair. "They're in too good a shape."

The spiked chair, or the 'Chair of Torture', was a heavy, solid wooden chair that resembled a crude throne of sorts. The seat, backrest, armrests, and leg rests were covered in sharp iron spikes at least an inch long. There were several dozen spikes or more covering the frightening chair. Iron wrist and ankle shackles were bolted to the chair, while leather straps were used for the neck and waist, keeping the intended victim tightly seated.

"This one is really intense," Randall announced, even though no one asked. "The unfortunate soul, who was often naked, was strapped into the chair, their body weight pressing against the spikes. The executioner would often leave the prisoner strapped to the seat for hours or even days."

His glee at telling tales of torture got him several looks from the women.

"For quicker results, the executioner could either tighten the straps or place weights on the prisoner's lap. The really crazy part was that the spikes were just long enough to puncture skin and muscle but short enough not to kill the victim right away."

Clair glared at her boyfriend. "You know you're a sick freak, right?"

"Me?" Randall announced with surprise. "I never tortured anyone."

Eva touched one of the chair's spikes and pulled her hand back in surprise. Brandy stared at her friend, somewhat horrified by her reaction.

"Wow, that's surprisingly *sharp*," Eva muttered.

Randall picked up a sword and examined it. "You wouldn't think they would be," he remarked, then looked a little closer. "But they certainly look real. Been used pretty hard, too."

Brandy approached and took the sword from Randall to examine it more closely. She could see it was scratched and dulled, as if it had seen a lot of action. Brandy quickly returned it to him, then looked at her friends, who were checking over the frighteningly realistic replicas. The entire room had her on edge with tiny goosebumps that refused to go away. The stretching rack had a large rectangular wooden frame that was ten feet long. Designed to inflict pain and dislocate joints through prolonged stretching, it was a gruesome device made of centuries-old wood and thick beam edges. There were iron shackles with heavy chains, which were fastened to the prisoner's ankles and wrists, attached to a stationary head roller and a movable foot roller. The foot roller was then turned by levers attached to a ratchet system that was slowly turned. To add to the not-so-charming therapeutic device's allure, there were three rows of spikes in the center of the rack under the prisoner's back that would tear into his flesh. It was painful just looking at it. Randall approached the spiked stretching rack and ran his fingers lovingly over it before turning to look at Brandy with a boyish grin.

"This one is a classic," Randall informed them. "The prisoner would first feel intense muscle strain. With continued turning, ligaments would tear, the shoulders, elbows, hips, knees, and spine would eventually dislocate with an unnerving *popping* sound." He chuckled softly, causing the women to tense immediately. "On this baby, the body could be stretched up to twelve inches or more over the course of hours or even days. Imagine the severe muscle damage, dislocation of virtually every major joint, all the ruptured tendons, and the massive internal bleeding."

When he realized the women were staring at him, he gave them an innocent look.

"What?" Randall scoffed.

Clair just shook her head and continued through the chamber. Randall was like a kid in a candy store, wanting to touch everything while grinning almost psychotically.

"I'll give you a thousand dollars for everything in the basement," Randall announced.

"Forget it, Randall," Brandy scoffed. "I'm not selling anything in this house."

"Now's no time to be greedy, Brandy," Randall remarked.

"I'm not being greedy," Brandy insisted. "I just don't know if I'm keeping the place or what I want to do with anything in it."

Randall ran his hand along the leather wrist straps and the unpleasant spikes. The wood appeared to be centuries old but in excellent condition. He jumped onto the portion of the table that was free of spikes and sat on it.

"Get rid of the spikes, and this could be a great little piece of furniture," Randall informed Clair while deviously raising his brows.

"Stop drooling over Brandy's antiques," Clair muttered. "It's damp down here. Let's go back upstairs and get drunk."

Randall jumped off the stretching rack and approached the wall loaded with different torture devices hanging from it. He picked up a spiked clamp, grinned, and looked at his friends.

"Wanna know what they used this for?" he asked almost slyly.

"No!" all four women cried out in unison.

Brandy shook her head and looked at Clair. "And you want to marry that?"

"We haven't set a date yet," Clair muttered. "I may reconsider."

Chapter 21

Midnight. All five friends sat at the felt-top card table, playing poker. Eva and Brandy were the only ones who weren't drinking, although Eva smoked a cigar alongside Randall. Judging by the pile of chips before her, Eva was clearly winning. After the initial shock of the dungeon wore off, Brandy was finally able to resume having a good time with her friends. It was possibly one of the best evenings they had together since they were of legal drinking age. In the near distance, lightning flashed, and thunder rumbled, but no one seemed to notice since they were laughing and enjoying the evening. More than the poker game itself, Brandy loved Raven's attention to detail. He refilled their drinks, emptied the ashtray, offered snacks, and catered to their every need. Well, within reason. Technically, Raven was just doing his job, but Brandy wanted to believe he found a way to enjoy the evening with them. When Raven headed to the kitchen for more snacks, Eva watched him leave and shook her head.

"I don't know what it is about that man," Eva remarked, "but he does something for me."

"He does have a certain quality," Paula remarked. "Kind of masterful, for a servant."

"Superior," Brandy added.

"I don't see what all the fuss is about," Randall remarked.

The four women laughed because it was really just the accent.

"Don't be jealous, Randall," Eva remarked.

"Be serious," Randall boldly announced. "I'm not jealous of a butler. You women are just living out some strange, demented fantasy. A servant can't be very exciting."

"He only has to be exciting for one hour," Eva remarked.

The women again laughed.

"I need more guy friends," Randall groaned.

Brandy tossed her cards on the table facedown after losing the last of her chips.

"I'm out," she huffed, then sighed and stood. "I'll be right back."

"Keep your hands off Raven," Eva called after her while grinning slyly. "He's mine."

"I'm going to the bathroom, if you don't mind," Brandy scoffed as she left the room.

After using the grand hallway powder room, Brandy headed toward the game room when she heard a woman's angry, raised voice from the kitchen. She changed direction to investigate. When she pushed open the swinging kitchen door, she witnessed Jana slapping Raven across the face before darting into the servant's quarters. Raven straightened, seemingly unfazed, and then turned, seeing Brandy standing in the doorway. He forced a tiny, embarrassed smile but didn't bother explaining.

"Is there something I can get for you, madam?" he asked.

"What was that all about?" Brandy asked, not waiting for him to offer an explanation.

"Just a mild temper tantrum," Raven casually replied. "The matter's been rectified."

Brandy stared at him somewhat suspiciously and cocked her head. If Raven made unwanted advances toward Jana, she wanted to know about it. Not that she had handled Eva's advances with much dignity, but Brandy was also drunk at the time.

"Maybe you should tell me anyway," Brandy informed him.

Raven appeared slightly uncomfortable but maintained his proud stance. "Jana's been, well, very *forward* with me, and I didn't appreciate her advances," he replied. "So I was forced to set her straight."

"So *she* slapped *you*?" Brandy asked, not sure she believed his story.

"I will admit, I'm a little rude when I'm cornered," Raven informed her. "I probably could have handled it with a little more dignity, as I had with Ms. Jericho last night."

He wasn't wrong. In her drunken condition, Eva practically threw herself at him, so it was possible Jana might have done the same. There was no doubt, Raven was a handsome man. Even Brandy had to admit she was attracted to him.

"I understand," she replied.

Brandy finally heard the raging storm outside and drifted into her own thoughts for a moment. The mansion was spooky enough without the classic 'dark and stormy night' to make it worse.

"Is there something troubling you, madam?" Raven asked.

"It's this house, Raven," she insisted, snapping back to reality. "There's something not quite right around here." She quickly looked back at him with an odd look upon her face. "Can you honestly say you haven't noticed anything strange about this place since you've arrived?"

"You don't really want me to answer that, do you?" he remarked with a tiny smirk.

Knowing he was referring to her behavior, she turned defensive.

"I'm serious," Brandy insisted. "I've never had these problems before, so it can't be me. Why is it I'm the only one who seems to notice these strange occurrences?"

Raven leaned against the counter behind him and studied her a moment. "Would you *really* like my opinion?" he asked.

Brandy hesitated, then nodded. She wasn't sure she'd like what he had to say, but she wanted to hear it anyway.

"Although I abhor gossip and particularly gossiping maids, Jana told me about your situation with your deceased father," Raven informed her. "I believe you've taken a perceived bad relationship and applied it to your father's kindness toward your best interest." He hesitated before continuing. "Simply put, you've resented your father for leaving, but now you feel guilty because it appears as if he really cared, and maybe you wish you could've known him."

Brandy stared at him, practically blindsided by his forensic analysis of her emotional trauma.

"Hmm, well, maybe there's something in what you've said," Brandy remarked. "But what's that got to do with the incidents within this house?"

"If the house were in some way defective or questionable, you'd be able to justify your continuing hostility toward your father," he reminded her.

"You're suggesting it's all in my head?" Brandy demanded. "That I somehow manifested all the strange things I've seen and heard?"

"That's exactly what I'm suggesting," Raven replied a bit too casually.

She was immediately offended. "I'm not imagining things!"

"I didn't say you were," he calmly replied. "I was merely offering a justifiable explanation."

Brandy studied him for a long moment in silence, wanting to lash out at him, but she couldn't deny he was probably right on some level. She shifted, now uncomfortable.

"You know, I haven't known any butlers, but you can't be typical," Brandy remarked.

"I'm so far from typical, they haven't found a name for it yet," he informed her, then seemed to reconsider. "Though 'bastard' comes up a lot."

Brandy appeared humored and laughed softly. "Maybe, but you do have a certain charm," she informed him.

Raven appeared pleased and offered a tiny smile. "Do you think so?" he asked.

They stared into each other's eyes for a long moment before Brandy caught herself blushing and looked away.

"I'd, uh, better join my friends," she announced while attempting to hide her smile before he read her mind.

The lights suddenly flickered and went out, startling Brandy. She gasped and felt every nerve in her body twitch.

"Power must be out from the storm," Raven informed her. "I believe I saw some candles here in the kitchen, and there are plenty in the dining room."

As Raven fumbled around the dark kitchen for some candles, a flash of lightning brightened the room for only a second and was immediately followed by a loud crack of thunder. It was so abrupt and loud, the house practically rumbled. Brandy's first instinct was to jump on Raven, but she folded her arms across her chest and rubbed her chilled shoulders in an attempt to self-soothe instead. She slowly moved closer to the window, stared out into the darkness, and listened to the pouring rain. There was another brilliant flash of lightning. Before she could even react, she saw something move past the window. Brandy gasped and jumped away from the window, crashing into Raven. Raven caught her arms, attempting to steady her until she regained her balance. Instead, she clung to his jacket.

"What's wrong?" he asked while fumbling with his lighter.

The small flame brightened the room enough to provide some comfort, though she refused to release his jacket, which she clutched tightly in her fists.

"Something moved past the window!" Brandy cried out while nodding toward the window.

Raven gently took her hand so she'd release his jacket and approached the kitchen door. Brandy clung to his hand and arm, following closely. He showed no fear and opened the door without hesitation. The rain continued to pour down in the darkness as the storm raged, but nothing moved. Both stared outside into the darkness for several minutes without seeing anything. Raven finally shut the door and turned to face her while she still clung to his hand and arm.

"I didn't see anything," he informed her.

Brandy abruptly released him and became immediately disgusted. "I'm not surprised," she scoffed.

"Ms. Holloway --" he announced delicately, but she abruptly cut him off.

"Don't you dare patronize me," she snarled, then spun and attempted to storm from the room. Brandy slammed into the heavy table and cursed loudly.

"Are you okay?" Raven asked with a little more concern in his tone.

"Fuck off!"

Chapter 22

The game room was engulfed in darkness as all four of Brandy's friends remained around the poker table, barely able to make out the silhouettes of one another.

"Okay, whose hand is that?" Eva snarled.

"Sorry," Randall announced. "I was looking for my lighter."

"Touch my chips again, and we'll find some use for those torture devices in the basement," Eva snarled at him.

"Please, don't give him any ideas," Clair muttered.

Randall chuckled, and a flame appeared from his lighter, brightening the entire table. All four remained sitting around the table as they had been before the lights went out, except now Eva's chips were slightly scattered. She immediately stacked and counted them.

"You guys have *no* sense of adventure," Randall announced. "You women need a little bondage in your lives."

Eva and Paula groaned and shook their heads.

"Get some candles, you pervert," Clair scoffed at her boyfriend.

"Where am I supposed to find candles?" Randall demanded.

"There were some on the dining room table," Paula informed him. "Raven lit them for dinner."

"Oh, yeah," Randall announced, then stood with his lighter flame. "Be right back."

Randall left the game room and made the short walk to the dining room with his lighter to brighten the way. Shadows were cast along the walls, seemingly following him. Randall entered the dining room and looked around the now dimly lit room. He could hear the rain pouring outside behind the wall of windows, although he couldn't see anything more than his own reflection. Lightning flashed, brightening the room and the outside world beyond the glass doors. A loud thunderclap immediately followed it. The storm didn't seem to be letting up at all. Randall approached the massive table and lit the three candles on the candelabra in its center. The lightning again flashed, catching Randall's attention. He saw something move outside, beyond the glass doors, but it was too dark to make out.

A faint snort was heard just beyond the wall of windows. Randall hesitated, then picked up the candelabra, rounded the table, and approached the glass doors. His reflection, along with the candles, was reflected off the glass. Randall moved closer to the glass to peer outside. A large, glowing green eye stared back at him, followed by another loud snort, fogging up the window. Randall cried out, just about dropping the candelabra, and ran from the room. He nearly collided with Brandy and Raven, who had been in the hallway at the time. Randall jumped back in surprise, letting out a loud gasp. All of his candles were now extinguished from his brisk run.

"There's something out there," Randall cried out while pointing into the dining room. "It was huge!"

Brandy glared at Raven and raised an arrogant brow. "See, it's not just me," she scoffed.

§

Randall stormed into the game room, his lit candelabra in hand, looking angry and anxious. Brandy and Raven entered only a second or two after him.

"What took you so long?" Clair demanded.

"Didn't you hear me yelling?" Randall scoffed at his girlfriend. "Thanks for checking on me." He remained agitated while turning his hostility onto Raven. "I'm telling you, I saw something out there!"

The others were now staring at a clearly agitated Randall, and his death glare directed at Raven.

"I'm sorry, sir," Raven replied, "but I didn't see anything."

"He gets stupid when he drinks," Clair insisted, not taking his rant seriously.

"I know what I saw," Randall scoffed.

Eva handed him a drink, but he pushed it away with agitation.

"I'm not drunk, and I *did* see something!" Randall insisted.

"What's with this place?" Paula demanded. "Is everyone losing their minds?"

"Not me," Eva chirped.

"I think we should call it a night," Clair remarked with a soft sigh.

"Could we at least finish our poker game?" Eva pouted. "I was winning."

Chapter 23

Brandy stood by the open balcony doors in the master bedroom, staring into the darkness overlooking the garden. She would have gone outside, but the heavy rain was hitting the balcony. The lightning flashed, briefly brightening the sky. She saw a white object in the garden, but it wasn't the fountain, and the horse statue was black marble. When the lightning flashed again, Brandy squinted to see if she could make out the object. There was a knock on the door, startling her. Brandy jumped and looked back into the room, feeling her heart pounding. She took a quick, deep breath as she tried to relax.

"Come in."

Raven entered the master bedroom carrying a candle on a fancy candlestick. "I've escorted your guests to their rooms," he informed her. "Will there be anything else, Ms. Holloway?"

"Come here, Raven," Brandy announced, still feeling a little anxious about what she'd seen in the garden. "Take a look at the garden. Do you see the statue of a woman out there?"

Raven approached the balcony doors, paused just behind her, standing unusually close, and stared outside into the darkness. Brandy was immediately aware of his closeness, almost to the point of distraction. When the lightning flashed again, she looked back into the garden.

"Yes, madam," Raven replied.

Brandy turned to face him, again realizing how close he'd been standing to her. She only let his closeness distract her for a moment.

"There wasn't a statue of a woman in the garden, just the horse," Brandy informed him.

Raven glanced past her to the balcony before returning his attention to her. "Statues don't just appear," he insisted. "You must be mistaken."

"I'm not mistaken," she retorted, then pointed to the garden behind her without looking. "Do you see the horse statue?"

Raven studied her a moment, then looked past her and waited until the lightning brightened the garden outside. He met her gaze while showing little emotion.

"I can't see it from here."

"That's because it's gone," Brandy insisted.

"Gone?" he asked, barely fazed. "Gone where?"

"I don't know," she replied as her anxiety spiked. "It just vanished."

"That's not possible, madam," Raven insisted while staring into her eyes through the candlelight. Something changed in his expression. "It's possible you have a mild concussion." He indicated the bench at the foot end of the bed. "Have a seat on my examination table."

"It's not a concussion," she insisted with a groan. "The same thing happened before I fell."

"Madam," he announced almost sternly. "Please humor me."

Brandy groaned, almost defeated, and sat on the bench. Raven sat on the bench beside her, partially turned, facing her, and placed the candlestick on the floor near their feet. He gently touched her face and gazed into her eyes. The light from the many candles around the room created a romantic backdrop, and Brandy couldn't deny she was actually enjoying his 'bedside manner'. Although she knew he couldn't properly check for a concussion without a flashlight, Brandy wasn't about to call him out on it. His touch again sent tiny shockwaves of excitement through her body, and she desperately wanted him to kiss her. Somehow, she felt his kiss would make everything better. Brandy couldn't wait any longer for him to make a move. She placed both hands on his face and kissed him with overwhelming urgency. There was no hesitation. Raven gathered her into his arms, pulled her against him, and returned the wildly passionate kiss. Brandy suddenly ached for him. She'd forgotten everything in that moment, wanting nothing more than this man taking her here and now. His kiss made her almost dizzy yet unusually relaxed. Raven broke off the kiss, recoiling with embarrassment.

"Forgive me," he announced softly while picking up the candle as he quickly stood. "I apologize for my behavior."

Brandy stared at him a moment, almost dumbfounded. "Your behavior?" she asked with surprise. "I kissed you."

"You've had a long, stressful day, Ms. Holloway," he announced almost without emotion. "You'll feel better in the morning. Goodnight, madam."

With that, Raven left the room. Brandy stared after him with astonishment. She couldn't believe the first time she'd ever made a move on a man, and he just walked away as if nothing had happened. If nothing else, he cured her paranoia, but it was now replaced with sexual frustration.

§

Raven carried a battery-powered lantern and a large black umbrella through the pouring rain across the garden. Despite the brightness of the lantern, it barely lit up the area surrounding him, yet he somehow managed to find his way with little difficulty. He walked several yards to the left of the fountain and paused on the path. Despite not seeing it from the master bedroom balcony, the horse statue remained exactly where it was supposed to be. There was a low snarl just beneath the bushes not far from the horse statue, but Raven couldn't hear it above the pouring rain. Raven approached the statue, unaware of the snarling sound and the glowing eyes coming from the bushes not far from him. He hesitated, then touched the statue. Something suddenly rustled within the bushes, catching Raven's attention. He directed his light toward the bushes, but there was nothing but darkness beneath the old, thick bush. Raven stared at the bush a moment longer, then scanned the dark garden.

The statue of a woman he'd seen from Brandy's bedroom wasn't anywhere within the garden. Raven's eyes strayed past the old gardener's workshop in the distance near the garage, and he seemed lost in thought for a moment. He finally headed along the path toward the fountain. Once he reached the fountain in the center of the garden, rather than turning onto the path leading back to the house, he turned off the lantern and collapsed the umbrella, setting both on the edge of the fountain. Raven casually walked through the pouring rain toward the gardener's workshop, not caring that he was immediately drenched. Once he reached the workshop, he barely paused to open the door that no longer appeared to be locked and entered the dark building. He barely got through the door when it slammed shut behind him.

Chapter 24

Clair nuzzled the pillow beneath her head while clearly naked and pleasantly rumpled beneath the sheets. Clair's guestroom had a similar layout, windows, and walls as the master bedroom, except on a smaller scale, which was still possibly bigger than Brandy's entire apartment. The guestroom was also decorated in deep purple. There were purple satin pillows, sheets, and bedspread, as well as two large purple velvet antique chairs and a purple throw rug in the center of the room. The tall queen-sized bed had a sculpted black headboard and a slightly shorter sculpted black footboard. The tall and long dressers, both black, matched the bed's details. Despite the elegant crystal chandelier, the room had the same creepy vibe as the master bedroom. When Clair reached across the bed, Randall wasn't there. She opened her eyes and saw her boyfriend buttoning his shirt. She clutched the sheets to her naked body, slowly sat up, and grinned almost seductively.

"Where are you going?" she asked. "I thought we'd get a little nap in before round two."

"You know I can't sleep during thunderstorms," Randall reminded her. "I thought I'd play some pool until the storm passes."

Clair returned to the mattress, barely pulling the sheet over her, and nestled the pillow while maintaining her smile. "Don't be gone too long," she cooed.

Randall grinned, leaned across the bed, and kissed her quickly but warmly on the lips. "Keep the sheets warm," he announced. "I'll be back in an hour."

Clair smiled and giggled. "If you're not, I'm starting without you," she warned him.

Randall chuckled, then took his lit candle and headed for the door. Clair maintained her sweet smile until he shut the door behind him.

§

Randall took a moment to look up and down the second floor hallway. Each direction seemed to have an adjoining corridor, making it difficult to tell which was the quickest route to the main stairs. It was an old house with a strange setup and a never-ending corridor. He finally decided to head right, hoping that was the correct way. If not, he would end up taking an unintended tour of the entire mansion via the kitchen stairs. Thankfully, he'd made the right choice and found the massive grand staircase. He headed down the stairs in his bare feet, taking each step a little slower than usual. The candle didn't provide nearly enough light, and he didn't want to miss a step. Although taking the steps more slowly made reaching the bottom seem like an eternity. Randall finally reached the bottom when he saw a pair of glowing green eyes reflecting in the glass of the grandfather clock, glistening in the candlelight. He gasped at what he thought he saw and took a quick step back, striking the broad banister at the bottom of the staircase. His candle extinguished from his sudden movement, as well as a slight draft that he'd felt a second before.

Randall fumbled with his lighter, trying to light the candle with trembling hands. He finally lit the candle and looked up to find Raven standing in the darkness, only a couple of feet from him. Randall let out a startled yelp and took a moment to regain his composure.

"Damn it, Raven," Randall cried out. "You scared me!"

"Sorry, sir," Raven announced, although he didn't seem the least bit sorry as he placed his hands in the pants pockets of his clean, dry suit. "I thought everyone was in bed."

"I couldn't sleep," Randall informed him, then looked around suspiciously. "What were you doing roaming around in the dark?"

"The battery in my lantern died," Raven replied, then managed a tiny shrug. "I have excellent nighttime vision and can see well enough to find my way around."

Randall accepted the answer, although he remained slightly suspicious. "Oh," he replied, then hesitated before finally relaxing. "Since you're up, would you care to play a game of pool?"

"No, thank you, sir," Raven replied. "I was just going to make rounds before turning in for the evening. Do you require anything else?"

"Uh, no, thanks," Randall replied, seeming uncomfortable with the whole 'servant' thing. "I'm good."

"Very well," Raven announced with a slight bow. "Goodnight, sir."

Raven continued past Randall and headed up the stairs at a brisk pace while somehow making little sound. Randall watched Raven turn past the landing and head up the second flight of stairs while requiring little light to find his way. Randall remained somewhat suspicious of the butler, but quickly cast his thoughts aside and headed directly for the dungeon basement door without a second thought.

§

Randall entered the torture chamber, despite his bare feet on the cold stone, and examined the antique torture devices and weapons with great interest. He picked up a broadsword and held it to the candle now on the display counter.

"Replicas, my ass," he muttered.

Within the nearly silent room, he heard a faint grinding sound. Randall tensed, looking away from the sword, and glanced around the creepy room. The candle didn't provide nearly enough light to see much more than shadows surrounding the objects of torture and destruction. He returned the sword to its wall mount and picked up his candle. It was then that he noticed several old candles positioned around the room. Some were attached to the wall on iron mounts, while others were on standing mounts. Randall lit several candles, which brightened the room considerably. He set his candle on a small table near the massive Iron Maiden and inspected the torturous device. Although carefully restored, many of the spikes showed signs of rust, particularly at the base. Randall was fascinated by the medieval piece and easily pictured how it worked and what the end result would be for the unfortunate prisoner.

The grinding sound was again heard, echoing loudly within the chamber. Randall whirled around and scanned the room. Despite not seeing anything that would have caused the horrific sound, his eyes settled on the stretching rack. What he heard was possibly the sound the torture device would make while inflicting pain upon its victim. Randall drew a deep breath, picked up his candle, and approached the large wooden monstrosity. He studied the torture device with great interest, again considering the ancient machine's inner workings. Although painfully unpleasant, he was fascinated all the same. As he carefully studied the rack, Randall heard the faint, distant cries of a woman screaming. He was about to look around when it dawned on him. It appeared as if the sound was coming from the torture device itself. Randall took a step back and stared at the massive stretching rack, now a little unnerved.

A soft, painful moan was suddenly heard from across the room furthest from the door. He whirled around to his left and focused on the spiked chair with its leather straps. Whatever he'd heard, it almost certainly came from the chair. There was a loud, horrendous grinding sound to Randall's right. He whipped his head around and saw the wheel turn on the rack only a foot from him. Randall jumped back with a startled gasp. He had been certain he'd seen the wheel move, but he had to be seeing things. There was another moan from the spiked chair. Randall jumped and spun back to the chair. Blood rapidly seeped across the spikes and ran down the seat, dripping to the floor. Randall withheld his frightened gasp and backed away from the torture devices, moving closer to the entrance. The unmistakable clanking of armor was heard behind him.

Randall spun around, but there was nothing there. He could barely control his heavy breathing as he shot looks around the entire room, afraid to turn his back in any direction. A gust of air blew past him, extinguishing every candle within the room. Randall suddenly cried out and ran to the open chamber door, fumbling with his lighter.

Chapter 25

Brandy slept restlessly while tossing and turning in her overly large king-sized bed in the massive, dark, and empty room. She was plagued with one horrifying dream after another before a woman's faint scream suddenly woke her. Brandy gasped as her eyes opened, and she practically flew up in bed.

"Mom!" she cried out, uncertain if she'd actually heard the scream in her dream.

A dark figure moved within the sculpted headboard behind her, slowly pulling out of the headboard while reaching for her. Brandy tried to control her heavy breathing as she ran her fingers through her mussed hair. When she finally relaxed and collapsed onto the bed, the dark figure had vanished without her ever knowing it had been there. While she attempted to make herself comfortable, a large lump moved under the covers near her feet. Brandy felt something near her feet, then looked and saw the moving covers. As she opened her mouth to scream, a decayed hand sprouted from the mattress near her head, covered her mouth, and pulled her head harshly against the pillow. While gripping the squishy, rotting flesh on the hand over her mouth, she saw and felt several lumps moving beneath the covers. Brandy attempted to kick out, but cold, icy hands clutched her legs. She tore at the rotted flesh on the hand over her mouth, feeling goo and slimy flesh. Two more decayed hands erupted from the bottom sheet, grabbing her wrists and forcibly pulling her hands down, pinning them to the mattress as well.

Brandy attempted to scream, feeling the goo seeping across her lips while the foul stench of rotting flesh assaulted her senses. As she struggled in vain to free herself, ghostly shadows manifested and stalked the room, buzzing around her and the bed. She was beyond terrified and felt as if her heart would explode from her chest.

"Brandy," the hellish voices whispered, further frightening her.

The glass balcony doors flew open with a strong gust of air, cracking as they struck the doorstops but not shattering. A thick, dark gray fog rolled into the room and up the tall footboard of her bed. The fog seemed to vanish beneath the covers, now raised by something massive and not human. Brandy could feel something cold and almost slimy moving over her bare legs and up her thighs. The sensation was horrifying, chilling her as it moved up her body. Her heart pounded even harder as she thrashed against the rotting hands and arms pinning her to the bed while attempting to scream. Loud thunderous pounding was heard against her door.

"Ms. Holloway, is everything all right!" Raven called out.

Filled with hope, Brandy wanted to scream for Raven to help her, but the hand covering her mouth refused to let any sound escape.

"Ms. Holloway!" Raven again shouted, the doorknob violently jiggling.

Brandy then heard a loud, beastly snarl as the large lump swiftly changed direction, seemingly reacting to Raven's commanding tone, and moved quickly back down her legs to the foot end of the bed. It reappeared as thick fog and rolled rapidly from the room. The balcony doors slammed shut behind the fog with a loud bang.

"You won't get away so easily," the voice whispered close to her ear while she remained pinned to her bed by the decaying hands.

Brandy attempted another scream, although her effort was in vain. There was a loud crack from the bedroom door as the jamb splintered and the door flew open. The lumps beneath the covers restraining her legs and arms vanished along with the hand over her mouth. Brandy screamed and lunged from the bed, nearly losing her balance. She saw Raven standing in the doorway, having busted down the heavy door. He scanned the room, immediately spotting the cracked glass on the balcony doors. Brandy ran across the room and threw her arms around his waist, clinging to him while shivering. His arms immediately tightened around her, holding her close.

"What happened?" Raven asked while attempting to look at her through the darkness, but she refused to pull her head away from his chest, while practically on the verge of tears. "Are you all right?"

"There was something in my room," Brandy sobbed. "It tried to *hurt* me!"

Raven continued to scan the room, unable to peel Brandy off him for a closer inspection. When it proved futile, his hands firmly caressed her back, attempting to stop her from shivering.

"There's no one here," Raven informed her. "What was it? What did you see?"

"It was a ghost," she insisted without pulling her face from his chest. "A very *foul* ghost."

No matter how hard she clung to Raven, Brandy couldn't shake the cold feeling of that thing that chilled her to the bone, and the foul smell of rotting flesh still assaulted her senses.

"You can think I'm crazy all you want," she remarked with her face buried into his shirt, "but you are *not* leaving my side!"

"I won't leave your side," he gently insisted, then seemed to hesitate. "Ms. Holloway? What is that smell?"

§

Randall hurried into the game room and ran straight to the bar. He grabbed a bottle of whiskey with a trembling hand and filled the entire glass. Randall took two big swallows and immediately made a face before gasping and collapsing onto the barstool. As he raised the glass to his lips, he heard a loud splashing sound. Randall hesitated, lowered the glass, and cautiously scanned the vast room behind him. His eyes fell upon the hot tub in the back corner. The water in the Jacuzzi rippled, then flooded over the edge, and ran down the side, forming a small puddle on the floor. Randal immediately looked up to the ceiling. Obviously, something must have fallen into the hot tub, but there hadn't been anything attached to the ceiling. Something then moved within the tub, creating more ripples. Randall stared a moment longer before finally setting his drink on the bar and slowly approaching the hot tub.

A large tail fin suddenly appeared from the Jacuzzi, then disappeared with a splash and more rippling water. Randall stared for a moment with a mixture of confusion and curiosity before slowly easing his way closer for a better look. A mermaid suddenly appeared above the water and propped herself on the edge of the hot tub. The vision of beauty had long, golden hair with seaweed and gold woven through it. Her long hair just about covered her nearly perfect, naked upper body. Small gills were displayed below and off to the side of her ample breasts. The mermaid moaned with desire, beckoning him closer. Randall stared at her a moment, somewhat intrigued, and smiled at the beautiful creature. Obviously, it was all just his imagination. She smiled and beckoned him closer again, revealing large pearl rings on each finger. Randall's eyes then strayed to the gold coins fitted into a large necklace, hanging low against her cleavage. His eyes remained focused on what appeared to be authentic 18th-century Spanish doubloons. The gold coins captivated Randall, and he took a step closer for a better look. He suddenly paused, his smile fading, and took a quick step back.

"This *isn't* a dream," Randall muttered aloud.

The mermaid dove under the water, and her tail fin once again appeared, splashing water from the tub and across the floor. Randall couldn't be sure, but she seemed pissed. He backed up into the pool table, unable to take his eyes off the hot tub and what he had just witnessed, when he felt something wet beneath his hands. He spun toward the game table in time to witness the mermaid jumping from the depths of the table top, now rippled with green, water-like waves. She grabbed onto the edge of the game table, and her mouth opened to reveal several rows of sharp, shark's teeth. A long tongue shot from her mouth, latched around his neck, and easily plucked him from the floor and into her expanding mouth. Randall wasn't even able to scream as she swallowed him whole. She then splashed back into the rippling pool table and vanished.

Chapter 26

Brandy stood in the walk-through shower, with all five showerheads on full blast, dousing her body with hot water while she repeatedly scrubbed every inch with a loofah bath sponge. Once she finished, she squirted more liquid bath soap on the sponge and scrubbed some more.

"For the record," Raven announced not far from one of the shower openings just out of view. "I'm a little uncomfortable with this."

"You can quit in the morning," Brandy called out, her fear turning to anger. "Sue me. I don't care. You're not leaving this bathroom!"

"You don't have to worry about that," Raven replied. "But I could have waited outside the bathroom door. Give you a little privacy and maybe a little dignity."

"After what I just went through," she scoffed, still shaken by it. "Be thankful I didn't insist you come in here with me!"

There was a moment of silence from outside the shower area. Brandy was positive Raven was still out there, although oddly quiet.

"That's not the terrible burden you seem to think it is," Raven finally replied. "I'm less likely to be embarrassed with watching you shower than you would be knowing you put on a free show for the hired help."

Brandy hesitated a moment, considering his words. While the trauma of what happened was still fresh in her mind, she might feel differently in the morning if she had insisted Raven stand in the shower with her. Modesty be damned! Right now, she needed him close by, and if that meant he got a free show, so be it. She finally rinsed off nearly the entire bottle of liquid soap she'd used and shut off the shower.

"I'm glad watching me shower wouldn't have been too much of a hardship on you," Brandy replied while grabbing one of two nearby towels hanging on the rack not far from the entrance of the elaborate 'shower tunnel'.

She swiftly wrapped the towel around her wet body, then used the second towel to dry her hair as she approached the opening where Raven waited. He casually leaned against the wall not far from the entrance and immediately straightened when he saw her emerge from the shower area. He watched as she dried her hair with the second towel and lightly cocked his head.

"I'm not really sure if you want me to turn around or not," he remarked, his tone conveying his uncertainty, a side of him she hadn't seen until tonight.

"A ghost practically probed my body," Brandy informed him somewhat sternly. "I don't really care what you see or don't see as long as you're within spitting distance."

Raven offered a tiny, understanding smile along with a nod, then appeared hesitant while turning his back to her.

§

Raven stood in the hallway with his decorative candlestick and the single candle that dimly lit the second floor hallway. He watched as his employer pounded on the last of the three bedroom doors located within the same stretch of hallway. Brandy knew Raven was secretly judging her, but she needed to warn her friends even if he thought she was crazy. Eva, Paula, and Clair entered the hallway in their sleepwear, looking disheveled.

"What's going on out here?" Eva asked, hardly awake and not the least bit concerned that she stood before Raven in her oversized t-shirt that barely covered her panty line.

"What time is it?" Paula moaned while running her fingers through her mussed hair.

"Around two in the morning," Clair muttered and shook her head. "Why did you drag us out of bed?"

"She must be having another episode," Paula huffed.

"I know you're going to think I'm nuts, but this house *is* haunted," Brandy insisted while attempting to control her anxiety. "You're my friends, and you know I care about you very much; that's why I'm asking you to leave."

All three women rolled their eyes and moaned at Brandy's command.

"If you have to go insane, Brandy," Eva announced. "Please don't take us with you."

Paula patted Brandy on the shoulder. "Yeah, we'll talk more tomorrow when you're sober."

"We'll get you some help, I promise," Clair announced.

"You aren't listening to me," Brandy cried out as her friends were returning to their rooms. "This isn't just some cute little haunting. These specters are playing for keeps. Our lives could be in danger!"

All three groaned their responses and returned to their rooms. One of her friends even slammed the door. Brandy spun to face Raven.

"I'm not crazy," Brandy insisted, now agitated. "Something held me to my bed while a fog monster probed my body. You believe me, don't you?"

Raven stared at her somewhat sympathetically. "I know *something* happened in your room tonight," he replied.

Brandy groaned while casting her back against the wall near him. "I knew it," she cried out. "You don't believe me either!"

Raven approached, stood over her holding the lit candle between them, and met her gaze. "What I believe doesn't matter," he informed her. "We need to decide what *you* intend to do about it."

She stared at him, somewhat baffled. "I don't know *what* to do!"

"It might be best if I took you to the nearest hotel," Raven informed her.

"No! I'm not going to leave without my friends," Brandy insisted, then looked around when it suddenly occurred to her. "I didn't see Randall? Where is he? Maybe I can talk some sense into him."

"I seriously doubt that," Raven remarked. "When I saw him around midnight, he mentioned playing pool. I'd imagine he's in the game room."

"After what he saw outside of the dining room, he'll listen to reason," Brandy insisted.

Before Raven could offer any advice or insight, Brandy was already running down the dimly lit corridor. Raven groaned softly and hurried to catch up with her while managing to keep his candle lit. Brandy stopped short of the grand stairs, staring down them into the pool of darkness below. Raven caught up with her, refusing to run to keep up.

"Before you take a nasty tumble down the stairs, perhaps you should stay close," Raven informed her. "Spitting distance, remember?"

She cast a quick look at him, then eyed the dark stairs and the even darker landing below. "You don't believe me," she pouted while folding her arms across her chest and rubbing her chilled arms. "You think I'm having some sort of psychotic episode, just like my friends think."

Raven set his candle down on the nearby hall table, drew a deep breath, and then placed his hands on her shoulders, surprising her. He forced her to face him and meet his gaze.

"I may not believe in ghosts or haunted houses," he informed her, "but I don't think you're having a psychotic episode either. The only thing that matters right now is that you feel safe."

As Brandy stared into his eyes through the dim candlelight, she felt her body relax.

"I can and will protect you, Ms. Holloway," Raven insisted. "You just need to trust me."

Raven released her shoulders and held his hand out to her. She glanced at his extended hand and again met his gaze. Brandy uncertainly placed her hand in his and instantly felt comfort.

"Okay," Raven announced as he reclaimed his candlestick and gave her hand an affectionate squeeze. "Let's go downstairs and find your friend."

Brandy walked calmly down the first set of stairs to the landing while clasping Raven's hand. His ability to put her at ease was mind-boggling, but she was grateful for his calm amidst her madness. By the time they reached the bottom of the second set of stairs, Brandy was feeling a lot better and more 'in control' of her emotions. Despite that, Brandy was convinced the grand hallway never looked creepier than it did during the storm without lights. She clung to Raven's hand, again becoming more skittish. Despite her rising anxiety now that they were on the first floor, Raven remained calm. There was a faint glow coming from the game room, reassuring Brandy that everything would be all right. As they entered, they saw several lit candles but no sign of Randall.

"Perhaps he went to the kitchen for something to eat," Raven informed her.

Brandy looked around the room and shook her head nervously. "I don't like this, Raven," she whispered.

He gently squeezed her hand, returning her attention to him. "Let's check the kitchen," Raven suggested.

Brandy clutched Raven's arm with her free hand and followed him from the room. They continued along the mostly dark hallway and then entered the dark kitchen. Raven released her hand and walked through the darkness with his candle, only brightening the area a little. There was still no sign of Randall.

"So much for that theory," Brandy muttered. "There's no place else he'd go."

Raven extended the candle to the open basement door and stared at it a moment, appearing curious. Brandy's eyes widened with horror at what he was possibly thinking.

"Oh, no!"

Something echoed deep within the basement beyond the partially open door. It sounded as if it were coming from the dungeon cells.

"You should wait here," Raven announced. "I'd better have a look down there."

Brandy grabbed his arm and stopped him from walking away. "Not happening," she informed him.

"Maybe Jana knows something. She's into this ghost stuff."

"But I heard something in the--" Raven began.

Brandy pulled him toward the servant's hallway and away from whatever it was he thought he heard in the basement.

"Don't care," Brandy informed him while pulling him along. "Not happening."

Chapter 27

Clair slept peacefully in her bed, curled beneath the sheets, despite being abruptly woken less than an hour earlier to Brandy's psychotic episode. Something caused her to stir, but she didn't know what had woken her.

"Clair!" Randall called out, sounding almost distant.

Clair's eyes popped open, and, with some disorientation, she looked around the mostly dark room but didn't see him.

"Randall?"

There was a light tapping on the glass balcony door, but it was too dark outside to see who was there. Clair crawled out of bed and wearily shuffled to the balcony doors. Randall stood outside on the terrace, soaking wet and shivering.

"Clair, let me in," he cried out with a sense of urgency.

Clair stared at him with confusion, then unlocked and opened the glass doors.

"What are you doing out there?" she demanded, not even sure how he got onto the balcony in the first place.

Randall blankly stared at her for a moment without stepping inside. His skin and flesh suddenly melted away from his face, exposing his skeletal frame. Clair screamed in terror and attempted to slam the glass doors. A heavy fog suddenly rolled in, keeping the doors from closing as Randall evaporated into it. Clair again screamed and jumped back as the fog rolled around her legs, while fog hands reached out and tried to grab her ankles. Clair screamed and jumped around, attempting to evade the fog hands wanting to detain her. A shadowy figure rose behind her while the frightening fog preoccupied her. She screamed frantically and finally pulled free from the 'fog hands', then spun around, coming face-to-face with a fog-like human figure. Clair screamed and jumped backward. The large, menacing figure lunged for her and swiftly wrapped around her, circling her entire body. The force of the fog threw her into the dresser just near the balcony doors.

Clair screamed hysterically and fought the fog arms that wrapped around her body like a large python. Eva's voice was suddenly heard through the shared wall from the bedroom next door.

"Clair? Are you all right?" Eva called out through the wall.

The fog swiftly evaporated and disappeared at the sound of Eva's voice calling to her. Clair clung to the dresser behind her for support while panting and staring at the once more empty room. Clair held her breath, breathed a sigh of relief, and then bolted for the door.

"Eva!" she called out, just about reaching the bedroom door.

The fog suddenly rolled out from under the bed and circled her legs, swiftly ensnaring her, and pulling her legs out from beneath her. Clair fell forward onto the floor with a loud thump and a terrified scream. As the fog engulfed her entire body, Clair flipped onto her back and frantically beat at the fog figure clinging to her. As the skin and flesh started melting from her face, she screamed. Eva threw open Clair's door and stepped into her room in time to see the thick fog swiftly roll out the balcony doors, leaving a ghostly image of Clair's horrified face and her arms reaching out to Eva. Eva ran across the room to the balcony as the fog dissipated, taking Clair with it. As Paula ran behind Eva onto the balcony, Eva stared outside into the darkness, uncertain what she'd actually seen. The rain continued to pour down with no sign of their friend.

Chapter 28

Raven knocked on Jana's bedroom door loudly enough that she should have answered right away, yet it seemed as if it took forever for her to respond. The door finally opened, revealing a weary, barely awake maid. Jana's bedroom in the staff wing was far smaller than any of the guestrooms on the second floor, but was still bigger than Brandy's apartment bedroom. The staff room didn't lack color and had the same gothic vibe. Although the floor had light to medium gray carpet rather than hardwood flooring, the rest of the room was either red-orange or black. The walls were a red-orange, as was the velvet material on the small, decorative chair with a black wood frame. The end table, dressers, and bedspread were black, while the headboard had a black frame with red-orange satin padding. It was almost surprising that the same gothic vibe spread into the staff quarters as well.

"Is something wrong?" Jana asked, appearing concerned, considering the hour.

"I know it's late," Raven remarked. "But we needed to talk to you."

"Something's happening in the house," Brandy announced while practically pushing Raven aside. "A fog monster attacked me."

Although she didn't see it, she could hear Raven's internal groan at Brandy's bluntness to a delicate situation that may or may not have happened.

"Fog monster?" Jana gasped, horrified, and then shook her head. "Ghosts don't attack the living. You must be mistaken. What's a fog monster?"

"We need to leave here. Now. Tonight," Brandy insisted. "You have to help me convince my friends to leave as well. We're all in grave danger."

"They can't hurt you, Ms. Holloway," Jana informed her. "They're just ghosts. You shouldn't worry yourself."

Brandy stared at her with surprise. Jana was the one person she was counting on for support. "You don't believe me either?"

"Well, it's just that you're describing things I've never seen before," Jana replied, now wide awake. "Ghosts just don't do those things."

Brandy dropped her head into her hands and groaned loudly in frustration. "I can't believe no one will listen to me." She spun to face Raven. "Why won't any of you listen?"

Raven smiled timidly at Jana. "Sorry to have disturbed you."

Jana nodded and shut her bedroom door.

Brandy cast her back against the hall wall. "You think I'm nuts," she huffed. "Admit it."

"I never said that," Raven insisted. "Just because I don't believe ghosts are haunting this house, that doesn't mean I don't believe in the supernatural." Raven placed his arm around her shoulder. "I'll take you back to your room."

She suddenly pulled free from him and backed away with her eyes wide in fear. "Oh, no! I'm *not* going back to my room!"

"It's okay, Ms. Holloway," Raven insisted. "I'll stay with you." He again placed his arm around her shoulder and held her against him while guiding her along the staff wing corridor to the kitchen. "Nothing will happen to you."

"I doubt that you'd be able to protect me against what came into my room," Brandy muttered, defeated. "How can you fight something you can't see?"

"I have more than one trick up my sleeve. You need to trust me, Ms. Holloway," Raven announced. "We'll search the entire house in the morning when it's light, if you'd like. Perhaps we'll even find an explanation for all of this."

"Maybe we should call the police," she countered.

"And tell them what?" Raven asked, eyeing her suspiciously. "You suspect your house is haunted? Some fog monster attempted to eat you? They'll lock you up for sure."

"Then maybe I'll call someone else," Brandy informed him.

"Whom?"

"My father's friend," Brandy insisted with renewed hope. "He may know something about what's going on here."

"Either way," Raven insisted. "It'll need to wait until morning."

By the time they entered the kitchen, Brandy was suddenly aware of Raven's arm securely around her shoulder, holding her to his side. She stopped him by the island counter and turned to face him, ensuring he'd drop his arm to avoid an unintended embrace.

"If you don't intend to quit in the morning, I assume you'll be asking for a raise," Brandy remarked, then managed a tiny smile. "I'm not usually like this. I really wanted to make a good impression on you."

"You have, Ms. Holloway," he replied in a soft and gentle tone while staring into her eyes.

"You stood in the bathroom while I showered for over twenty minutes, you saw me in nothing but a towel, and I ruined your entire night's sleep with my insanity," she informed him. "Do you think *maybe* you can call me by my first name?"

Raven was oddly silent for a moment while staring back at her. "I have a small confession to make," he remarked. "Seeing you in nothing but a towel kind of made up for the rest of the night."

Brandy stared at him, slightly surprised by the admission, then almost giggled before hiding her smile and looking away.

"Well," she announced with a soft sigh, then gently smoothed his tie before again meeting his gaze, unable to hide her smile any longer. "You obviously don't get out enough."

"Actually, I'd seen enough of the world when I was younger," he informed her. "In the shower with an attractive young woman at this point in my life is precisely where I'd like to be."

Brandy felt her cheeks instantly flush, but forced herself to maintain eye contact. "Stick around for a couple of weeks, and we'll see if that position opens up."

Raven could no longer hide his humored smile, then chuckled softly while gently brushing a stray lock of hair from her face.

"A fantasy for another day," he informed her, then straightened and turned serious, taking her hand in his. "Tonight, I just want you to feel safe, so I'm going to take you upstairs to the room we'd freshened for your friend that never showed. You're going to get a few hours' sleep, and I'll post guard alongside your bed until morning. After breakfast, I'll search the entire estate and find you some answers." He smiled warmly. "Okay, *Brandy*?"

"Your terms are acceptable," she replied.

Raven raised her hand to his lips and affectionately kissed it without taking his eyes off hers. She couldn't deny that his sensual manner, along with the erotic sensation, drove her instantly insane. As he lowered her hand while caressing it, his eyes remained focused on hers. Despite being completely out of character for her, Brandy wanted this man, even if it were just a meaningless fling.

"If you want me to feel truly safe," Brandy announced somewhat timidly, attempting to channel her inner Eva. "You could guard me more closely from within my bed."

Brandy couldn't believe she actually said it! There was no coming back from it now. She made the first move and put sex on the table. Brandy gave him the power to reject--

"If that would make you feel safer," Raven replied in possibly the sexiest tone Brandy had ever heard. "But I won't take advantage of you in your vulnerable condition."

Brandy considered the comment, then eyed him. "Not even a little?"

Raven hid his smile and had to look away. "Well, things happen," he replied.

"It *would* make me feel safer," she assured him.

He hesitated only a moment before pulling her into his arms, his lips seeking hers. Brandy immediately sank against him and returned the warm but passionate kiss. Raven pulled away just as quickly, seeming reluctant to look her in the eyes while taking her hand in his.

"My days of meaningless flings are behind me," he gently admitted, then finally met her gaze. "I'm not saying I wouldn't love to ravish you because that would be a lie. I just--I need it to be more. I need to protect my heart as much as I need to protect you."

Brandy stared at him a moment, attempting to read between the lines. "So--you want to get to know me better *romantically*?"

Raven stared into her eyes. "Yes, that's what I'm trying to say," he replied. "There are things you would need to know about me and my past. Important things that you would need to accept before things go too far."

Brandy stared at him a moment before smiling. "I would love to get to know you better," she announced. "Honestly, that would have been my first choice. A meaningless fling was the consolation prize." She managed a tiny chuckle. "It's been a long time since I've even been interested in a guy."

"I'm glad to hear," Raven announced, then hesitated. "I mean, that you want to get to know me better, although I'm not too bothered that you haven't been interested in many guys." He gently cleared his throat. "I'm going to shut up now."

"Since I'm obviously not getting any sleep tonight anyway," Brandy began. "Why don't we hang out and get to know each other better?"

"I'm still up for cuddling while we do that," Raven informed her. "If the offer still stands."

Brandy held back her laugh. "Absolutely," she replied. "I'd enjoy that very much."

Raven again kissed her hand, then guided her into the grand hallway and toward the stairs. "Believe me, we have a lot to talk about," he insisted.

Chapter 29

Raven and Brandy approached the grand stairs by the light of Raven's candle. It was then that they heard screaming from the second floor. Eva and Paula thundered down the steps, nearly colliding with Raven and Brandy. Both women, who had hastily dressed, slid to a halt and began shouting in unison.

"Brandy!" they cried out while grabbing Brandy's arm. "Clair's gone!"

"We heard her screaming," Paula announced.

"We went into her room," Eva cried out. "She's gone!"

"What do you mean, gone?" Raven asked, attempting to make sense of their ramblings. "Where did she go?"

"The balcony doors were wide open," Eva insisted. "There was this fog." She placed her hand on her chest. "I swear, the fog took her away!"

Brandy suddenly gasped in horror and shot a look at Raven. "It was the same fog that came after me in my room," she informed him, feeling her paranoia spike.

Raven immediately gathered the three women together and herded them into the nearby library. All three were now nervously pacing, feeding off one another's fears, and ready to explode. Raven stopped in the doorway and eyed them.

"Wait here and don't leave," Raven instructed in a firm tone. "I'm going to look around her room."

"Don't leave us!" Paula cried out.

"I'm coming back," Raven insisted. "Stick together and don't leave this room."

"Raven," Brandy protested with concern, pleading with her eyes. "Please, don't go."

"I'll be fine," Raven reassured her. "I'm coming right back, I promise."

After Raven left the library, shutting the door behind him, the three women looked at one another with increasing concern.

"We're so sorry we didn't believe you," Paula gasped while rubbing her chilled shoulders.

"What's going on around here?" Eva demanded, her fear turning to anger. "What kind of house did your father leave you?"

"It's some sick and twisted revenge," Brandy informed her. "I should've seen it from the beginning. He never wanted anything to do with me, but then he leaves me his entire estate?" She shook her head. "It was too good to be true because it was. He was probably some sick psychopath, and he did this to me just to torture me."

"Maybe he's not really dead," Paula suggested as her eyes widened. "Like one of those crazy movies. He faked his death, and now he's inside the house, intending to kill us all one at a time."

"I'm going to call that man who knew my father," Brandy informed them.

"What good will that do?" Eva demanded. "If he was your father's friend, he's not going to help us. Maybe he's even behind all of this."

"Attorney Rockwell told me my father cut his own son out of his will," Brandy informed them. "What if his son, my half-brother, is here in this house? What if this is all an elaborate scam to get me out of the house so Ford can inherit? There's no telling what my half-brother might do to get what he wants."

Brandy hurried to the library door with both her friends on her heels.

"Raven said to wait here," Paula reminded her.

Eva suddenly stopped, a look of horror crossing her face. "What if Raven *is* your brother?" she gasped.

Brandy hesitated, then turned to face Eva with a somewhat shocked look before shaking it off.

"Don't be stupid," Brandy huffed, then turned back toward the door while grimacing. "If he is, I'm going to need a lot of therapy."

Brandy left the library and hurried across the dark hallway to the study with Paula and Eva on her heels. Once they entered the study, they lit several candles, considerably brightening the room. Eva closed and locked the door behind them just to be safe. Brandy grabbed the phone on the desk and opened the nearby phonebook. She found the number and dialed it.

"That poor man's going to think you're absolutely wacko," Paula muttered while pacing the room.

Brandy held the phone to her ear as she waited, looking at her friends. "My father supposedly kept a leather-bound journal," she informed them. "Why don't you see if you can find it?"

Paula and Eva began searching the room while Brandy remained on the phone waiting for a response to her call.

"No one can help you now," a creepy voice on the phone whispered into her ear, instantly chilling her.

Brandy cried out and dropped the phone, unable to shake the horror of hearing that voice in her ear. Eva and Paula ran back to her and looked around.

"What's wrong?" Eva asked.

"It was the same voice that threatened me earlier tonight," Brandy gasped.

Eva picked up the discarded phone and nervously placed it to her ear. She hesitated, then looked at Brandy.

"There's no dial tone," Eva informed her. "This phone doesn't even work."

"I swear it was working only a minute ago," Brandy announced.

"We need to get out of this house," Paula insisted, now trembling in addition to her pacing.

"Just stop it," Eva cried out as she slammed the phone down and glared at Paula. "You're not helping!" There was a brief silence before Eva eyed her friends. "We should search Raven's room. If he is your brother, there may be some evidence of it."

"He's not my brother," Brandy insisted while obsessively raking her fingers through her still damp hair. "Ford wants the journal, so we need to find it first. It might be the only thing that'll keep us alive."

Just then, they heard Clair's faint scream from somewhere within the house. All three ran to the study door that Eva opened. They heard the scream again and looked down the hallway, trying to trace its source. Paula grabbed a candle and joined them in the corridor. When they heard Clair screaming again, Brandy pointed down the hall toward the kitchen.

"This way!" Brandy cried out.

All three ran down the long hallway and entered the kitchen. Brandy, who had been in the lead, nearly collided with Jana. All four women screamed in response.

Jana clutched her chest and breathed heavily. "You scared me," she cried out, then became alarmed. "I heard screaming. Was it you?"

"No, we heard it too," Eva informed her. "It sounded like our friend, Clair. We have to find her!"

"Where's it coming from?" Paula asked.

The house was eerily silent as all four looked around, then at one another while waiting. The screaming was no longer heard. A moment passed when they heard a faint, metallic echo. All four slowly turned their heads and looked at the now closed basement door. It appeared to glow and bulge at the seams.

"Oh, no," Paula cried out while shaking her head. "I'm not going down there!"

"The torture devices," Brandy gasped, now horrified. "Clair!"

Brandy ran for the basement door despite what she saw. Eva cursed under her breath, then hurried after her, now with her own candle. Paula reluctantly groaned and followed them with the second candle. Jana hesitated a moment, looked around the dark and creepy kitchen with some uncertainty, then hurried after them. Brandy paused before the haunted door that seemed to breathe and hesitantly reached for the doorknob. As she just about touched the knob, the door immediately flew open, away from her and striking the doorstop with a thunderous crack. All four women jumped back with startled screams. Both candles were extinguished by the gust of wind coming from the stairwell, leaving them in near darkness. While Eva frantically fiddled with her lighter, trying to light both candles, the women realized the glowing green light was gone. They were left with just the incredibly creepy stone steps leading into an actual dungeon of a haunted house.

Paula handed Brandy her candle and indicated for her to lead the way. Brandy wanted to protest, but it was her house, and her mess. She held her breath a moment, then let it out, finding her courage.

"For Clair," she whispered, then crept down the steep stone steps with the three women following her.

Chapter 30

Raven entered Clair's dark bedroom with his candle guiding the way. The candle provided only minimal light, though it reflected off the glass balcony doors, creating distorted, almost ghostly images. Raven set his candle on the nearby dresser and inspected the room more closely. The bed sheets were pulled back without any indication of a struggle, the same as he had found in Brandy's room. The balcony doors stood open, allowing the sound of the pouring rain echo throughout the room. Raven approached the balcony, paused by the open doors, and looked outside. He lifted his head and sniffed the air, now somewhat curious by a smell other than the fresh rain. Raven approached the dresser closest to the balcony and glanced over it. There were deep fingernail scratches in the antique wood. He traced the scratches with his fingers and sank into thought.

While Raven was focused on examining the dresser, a grotesque and distorted creature's reflection was visible in the standing mirror a couple of feet behind him, but was unseen by the butler. The barely visible creature stepped out of view of the mirror as Raven straightened, keeping him from seeing it. Raven stood facing the dresser a moment while remaining deep in thought. A low yet vicious snarl was suddenly heard from nearby. Raven was alerted to the sound and immediately spun, but was too late. He harshly struck the dresser behind him as the beastly snarling continued.

§

When Brandy and Eva reached the bottom of the dungeon steps, they immediately froze and looked around. The entire basement dungeon had suddenly changed to something far worse than the creepy dungeon they had previously visited. Although the layout remained the same, the cell doors were rusted and stained with blood. The women distinctly heard the sound of dripping water, which explained why the floor was damp. The floor had a streak of blood down the corridor, as if something had been dragged to or from the torture chamber. All the torches on the walls were now lit, revealing massive cobwebs that held several fat, hairy spiders. Brandy saw the first fist-sized spider and immediately shivered. Several moans and faint screams were loudly heard from deep within the dungeon. Eva and Brandy could do little more than stare, unable to hide their looks of sheer horror. Paula and Jana stopped on the stairs just a few feet behind them, appearing equally horrified.

"Where the hell are we?" Paula asked, now clinging to her arms while shivering.

"It's the ghosts," Jana gasped, unable to tear her eyes from the far creepier dungeon. "They're trying to frighten us."

"It's working," Paula muttered, then attempted to go up the stairs.

Jana grabbed Paula's arm and forced her to stay with them. "They want to get us alone," she insisted. "We need to stick together."

"We should wait for Raven," Paula suggested.

"If Clair's down here, she may not have that much time," Brandy remarked as she shivered partially from the dampness but mostly from fright.

Brandy forced herself to walk along the medieval dungeon corridor. Her steps were slow and cautious. Somehow, the spiders seemed to be the less frightening part. Eva, Paula, and Jana uncertainly followed her, sticking together in a small cluster, clutching each other's arms. Dirty, grimy hands suddenly reached out of the cells through the bars and grabbed for the women. The three women screamed while Brandy jumped nervously to the opposite side, knocking a broadsword from the wall. The moans grew louder as more hands reached for them.

Brandy shut her eyes a moment and whispered, "This isn't real."

"Looks damned real to me," Eva muttered.

"Clair," Brandy finally called out and continued along the corridor.

There was no response other than moans and cries from within the cells. Eva followed Brandy from a distance while staring at the hands grabbing for her. Jana and Paula appeared to be frozen, clinging to each other, and didn't follow. There was a light from the partially open torture chamber door at the end of the corridor. Something within the room disrupted the light, casting a shadow in the torture chamber. Obviously, that was where they needed to go, but the thought was terrifying. Brandy and Eva looked back at Paula and Jana, who still hadn't moved. Once they reached the door, Brandy slowly pushed it open, flooding more light into the corridor. Brandy drew a deep, tense breath, held it, and then slowly entered the chamber. Mostly skeletal remains now occupied the room's once-empty antique torture devices with only a little gooey flesh and cartilage holding the bodies together. There were now several severely decayed bodies hanging from the many shackles lining the side wall.

Brandy and Eva slowly entered, horror on their faces at what they were witnessing. If Clair had been in the room, there wouldn't be enough of her left to identify. Eva clutched Brandy's arm and indicated the table not far from the stretching rack. It contained some of the old rusted tools they'd seen earlier, along with some new ones. All were covered in dried blood except two, which were drenched in fresh blood. The streak of blood from the corridor led to a small, bar-covered oubliette in the floor that hadn't been there before. Brandy's heart was now pounding at the thought of Clair possibly being in the pit, undoubtedly dead, with all the blood on the floor surrounding it. Unfortunately, they had to look. They had to be sure. Eva remained close to Brandy as they took two steps closer to the locked dungeon pit. The heavy torture chamber door slammed shut, and both women cried out as they spun around.

A severely decayed man jumped at them from where he'd been hiding behind the door. Eva and Brandy screamed and tried to leap out of its path. The decayed man grabbed Brandy and threw her across the damp dungeon floor. She rolled several times, struck the side wall, and crashed into the decayed bodies hanging from shackles on the wall. Their flesh and cartilage tore, and their gooey remains crashed to the floor alongside her. Brandy cried out and attempted to throw the rotting, foul-smelling body parts off her. The severed, decayed arms began moving while their hands tried to grab her. The incident in her bedroom suddenly came back to haunt her in vivid detail. Brandy scrambled to her feet and kicked two severed arms away from her. When she lifted her head, she saw the decayed creature standing directly in front of her.

"Run," Eva cried out to her friend while throwing open the door and bolting from the room.

It wasn't as if Brandy had any place to go. She was more or less trapped in the corner, not far from the spiked chair. The decayed man lifted a blood-stained axe, which had been on the table with the other tools of torture, and smiled evilly through yellow, rotted teeth. The creature swung the rusted weapon at Brandy. She screamed and dived out of the weapon's path, narrowly avoiding the spikes on the torture chair. With little maneuvering room, she ran directly into the stretching rack, striking the heavy device and definitely inflicting massive pain on herself. She just about fell on top of the decayed man, nearly torn apart while strapped to the gruesome rack. Brandy gasped at how close her face was to the partially torn, decayed man. The decomposed man suddenly opened his eyes and stared at her. Brandy screamed again and bolted upright.

The decayed creature with the axe slashed at her with his weapon. Brandy screamed and dived to the floor, out of the weapon's path. Instead, the axe struck the semi-torn man on the rack, the blade cracking his skull. Brandy scrambled to her feet and darted across the room toward the door, tripping over the dungeon pit and falling to the floor. When she looked behind her, the decayed creature was standing over her, prepared to chop her apart where she cowered on the floor. Brandy screamed and shielded her face, preparing for the pain of the small axe. Eva suddenly jumped through the doorway with the discarded broadsword from the corridor wall clutched in her hands. She swung and struck the axe in mid-air with her own blade. The metallic crack and Eva's scream were almost deafening.

Eva was sent down to one knee from the impact and the weight of her own sword. As Brandy scrambled to her feet, the decayed man pulled the axe back and swung again. Eva screamed and blocked the blade a second time, but this time, she was knocked to the floor from the powerful blow, losing her sword with a loud clatter. As one of the arms crawled closer to her, Brandy grabbed it by the wrist and swung, bashing the creature on the head. Unaffected, the beast turned and grabbed Brandy by the throat with his left hand while preparing to strike Eva with the axe in his right. Jana and Paula were suddenly heard screaming from within the depths of the corridor. A large black wolf appeared in the doorway of the torture chamber and snarled, its massive, bloodstained teeth exposed. The wolf suddenly lunged for the decayed man.

Eva scrambled across the floor on her backside while screaming at the entire scene as it unfolded. The creature propelled Brandy across the room, face-first, toward the open Iron Maiden before focusing its attention on the wolf. Brandy caught the edges of the Iron Maiden with both hands and stopped herself from falling inside. She stared with a horrified gasp at the bloodstained spikes only inches from her face. The wolf tackled the creature to the stone floor and sank its teeth into its throat, tearing and ripping with vigor. The creature exploded into hundreds of tarantulas, quickly scattering. Several hairy spiders ran across Eva, who was still on the floor. She screamed and sprang to her feet, batting her clothes. The wolf suddenly vanished before their eyes. Eva continued to scream and swat at her clothing, fighting the spiders that were no longer there. Paula and Jana ran into the room and looked around with terror in their eyes while Brandy grabbed Eva and joined them by the door.

"Let's get the hell out of this place," Paula cried out.

Eva reclaimed her discarded sword and clutched it. "I'm with you."

As all four ran from the room, the basement had now returned to its original state. Despite being back to its normal level of creepiness, all four didn't look back and ran for the stairs. Brandy suddenly stopped them at the bottom of the stairs.

"What about Clair and Randall?" Brandy gasped.

"*It* has them," Paula insisted while just about ripping the hair from her head as she violently ran her fingers through it. "We're no match for whatever's in this house!"

"Look, this isn't some trick to steal your inheritance," Eva insisted. "This goes way beyond normal. We don't even know that they're alive."

"We don't know that they're dead either," Brandy reminded her. "They're our friends."

"If the situation were reversed, do you think they'd come for us?" Paula asked.

There was a strange moment of silence. They pretty much knew the answer.

"I say we leave here and send the police back to look for them," Paula announced while trembling.

"She's right," Jana replied, unable to control her heavy breathing. "We can't beat this thing. You can't defeat the supernatural."

Chapter 31

All four women ran down the dark, grand hallway to the front door, barely able to see where they were going without their discarded candles. Brandy lagged behind and paused at the bottom of the grand staircase. She was having a difficult time leaving her friends behind while knowing they had simply vanished somehow, but she couldn't run out on Raven without at least telling him they were 'escaping'. When Brandy looked up to the staircase landing, she noticed something was 'off', but she didn't really take the time to think about it.

"Raven!" Brandy called up the stairs. "We're getting out of here! Drop whatever you're doing and get down here!"

There was no response, even though she yelled loudly enough that he would have heard her. Brandy glanced at the three women standing in the foyer before the front door.

"Come on, Brandy," Paula pleaded while frantically waving for her to join them. "He's on his own."

Brandy looked back at the stairs, unable to simply leave him 'on his own'. "Raven!"

"Screw him," Jana cried out, shaking her head. "We have to get out of here!"

Jana threw open the front door, revealing a thick fog that immediately rolled inside. Brandy looked back at the door and saw the all-too-familiar fog, instantly sending shivers down her spine. Eva and Paula were equally horrified at the sight. Only Jana hadn't witnessed the terror of the menacing fog.

"Close the door!" Brandy screamed.

Jana gasped and slammed the door, but it was already too late. As the fog engulfed poor Jana, Paula jumped back and collided with Eva. All three women could do little more than stare in horror as Jana screamed and batted at the fog clinging to her. Eva firmly grasped her sword and bravely took a step toward the terrified maid, prepared to battle it, when a fanged, fog mouth snarled and attempted to bite her. Eva screamed and jumped backward, colliding with Paula and Brandy. Jana let out a shrill shriek as she instantly turned to ice before their eyes. Paula screamed in horror while clinging to Eva's arm as all three stared helplessly at the woman now frozen solid. Jana's ice figure suddenly shattered and was met with more screams. The jagged, shattered pieces evaporated into the fog that rapidly seeped under the door and out of the house. All three women stumbled backward toward the staircase.

"She's gone!" Paula cried out, her eyes wide and horror-filled.

"We're trapped!" Eva screamed as she shifted her gaze around the mostly dark grand hallway.

Brandy grabbed her friend's arms. "Come on!"

"Where are we going?" Eva asked without protest and hurried to the staircase.

"We need to find Raven," Brandy informed them, now driven.

Paula suddenly stopped Brandy. "You're out of your mind," she cried out. "We don't want to go deeper into the house. We have to get out of here!"

"And how do we know he's not part of what's going on here?" Eva demanded.

"This isn't manmade, Eva," Brandy reminded her, defending Raven. "What part could Raven possibly have in this?"

"We need to stick together," Eva insisted, then looked at Paula. "We're going upstairs. Together."

"Yeah, like staying together has done us any good so far," Paula scoffed. "You're both insane."

"We're not getting out the front door," Brandy informed her friend. "If you have a better idea, I'd love to hear it."

Paula frowned her response. All three hurried up the stairs to the landing, then slowed before heading up the next flight to the second floor corridor. The women suspiciously eyed the large, stained-glass window, which showed only scenery and a castle in the distance.

"Am I crazy, or is there something missing from that window?" Eva muttered.

"Well, you're not crazy," Brandy replied.

Eva, Paula, and Brandy cautiously walked into the dark second floor hallway and found a set of candles in decorative sticks on a nearby hall table. Eva lit the two candles, which Paula and Brandy each took one, leaving Eva free to carry her sword, their only weapon, not that there weren't plenty of other swords hanging on the walls as decoration. As they crept down the corridor by candlelight, everything appeared quiet.

"This isn't good," Paula whispered.

"Remain alert," Eva remarked.

"Raven?" Brandy softly called out. "Raven!"

There was no response, although none were actually surprised. They paused before Clair's closed bedroom door and exchanged looks. Raven had been heading to Clair's room, but there was no telling what they would find behind the door. Paula and Eva then eyed Brandy, silently suggesting she go first since it was her quest. Brandy drew a deep, tense breath, then quietly turned the knob. Despite her best effort, the door couldn't have made any more noise if she had simply busted it down. Brandy held up the candle, brightening the large bedroom. Although the room appeared to be empty, there were huge bloody paw prints on the floor leading from the bed to the balcony. The glass doors were shattered, and several objects within the room were broken and scattered across the floor. The bloody paw prints then continued from the balcony into the bathroom. Brandy slowly entered the room, watching her corners and even looking behind the door. She didn't want another surprise as she had in the dungeon.

Eva uncertainly followed her and also looked around the room while clutching her sword. Eva suddenly grabbed Brandy's arm with a horrified gasp, startling her friend. Brandy jumped with surprise, then turned to see what had unnerved her friend. Eva anxiously pointed at a lump on the bed beneath the blood-soaked sheets. As both women slowly approached the bed, Paula stepped just inside the room and nervously clung to her candlestick, keeping watch on the dark hallway behind her as well. Brandy slowly reached for the sheet, grasped it with one hand, and yanked it back while simultaneously jumping away from the bed. Another decayed man lay on a heap on the bed, severely mauled by something. Brandy and Eva gasped and then exchanged looks.

"Do you think it's--?" Eva asked.

Brandy slowly shook her head. "No, it's not Raven," she insisted.

"He's not here," Paula whispered with increasing anxiety. "Let's get out of this place!"

"I'm with Paula," Eva announced and slowly shook her head. "Whatever's happened to the others has happened to Raven as well."

Brandy admitted defeat for the sake of her remaining friends. She couldn't risk their lives running around the house looking for Raven when it was possible he was already gone. They needed to find a way out of the house. All three hurried from the room and along the upstairs corridor, brightened only by the two candles.

"What's the plan then?" Paula asked. "How do we get past that fog? What if it's surrounding the entire house?"

"We have to make a run for it," Eva insisted while gripping her sword.

"And wind up like Jana?" Paula gasped, eyes wide with horror.

"Any better ideas?" Brandy asked with a defeated sigh. "We either run, or we hide."

"Somehow, I don't think hiding is much of an option," Paula muttered. "You can't hide from the supernatural."

Chapter 32

As Brandy, Eva, and Paula hurried down the grand staircase and into the main hallway, the sound of hoof beats and clanking metal echoed. A horse's loud snorting alarmed the women. All three spun in time to see a knight in silver armor on a white horse running toward them from the front door. It wasn't a ghostly apparition; it was very real. They turned to run in the opposite direction when another horse squealed. They looked toward the ballroom at the other end of the corridor and saw a knight in black armor on a black horse in the ballroom doorway. The black horse reared, then ran for the knight on the white horse. The women screamed and bolted out of the path of the knights with broadswords drawn, prepared to battle. When the knights clashed in the middle of the grand hallway, the black knight struck the white knight's shield and sent him toppling off his horse with a loud clatter.

The fallen white knight staggered to his feet with his sword in his hand and spun just in time to clash swords with the black knight on horseback. Brandy, Eva, and Paula watched the knights battle each other for a moment, somehow unable to turn away. The knight on the black horse swung harshly and suddenly decapitated the white knight. Paula screamed hysterically and backed into the nearby wall while Eva and Brandy looked at the fallen knight with horror, then saw that the helmet was empty. When they looked at the rest of the armor, it too was empty. The black horse reared up on command as the black knight celebrated his victory. When the horse landed, the knight grabbed Paula around the waist, plucking her off her feet. She screamed while being thrown over the front of the saddle. The knight then whirled the horse around and galloped for the ballroom. The doors opened as the knight rode toward them, while Eva and Brandy ran after him, screaming.

"No!"

Paula screamed hysterically, crying out for her friends, while attempting to free herself. Eva and Brandy ran into the ballroom behind the knight, then skidded to a halt and watched as the horse jumped into the large painting at the far end of the ballroom. The knight, his horse, and Paula vanished into the painting. Paula could now be heard screaming from somewhere deep within the house. Brandy and Eva ran to the painting and stared at the image of an English countryside with a castle in the distance. It was almost the same as the stained glass window on the grand staircase landing. Both touched the painting, but it was solid.

"Paula!" Eva gasped, then looked at Brandy, horror in her eyes. "What are we going to do?"

"We need to get help!"

"How?" Eva demanded. "Whatever is holding us here isn't going to let us out."

"I don't know how, but we have to get out of here," Brandy insisted while still studying the painting.

"What about the journal?" Eva announced, becoming animated. "If your father knew the house was haunted, maybe there's some way we can stop all of this."

"I tried looking for it but couldn't find it," Brandy insisted. "I don't know where else to look. I checked everywhere. His study, the library, and his bedroom."

"I certainly don't have any other ideas," Eva informed her. "Let's go to the study. Maybe there's a hidden panel, a secret compartment, or a hidden drawer. We'll tear the study apart if we have to."

As they turned and hurried back for the ballroom entrance, Brandy noticed both mounted knights on horseback were missing from their display on the opposite end of the room. Brandy and Eva ran from the ballroom and hurried along the dark grand hallway toward the study. It only took a second for Brandy to realize that every suit of armor was now missing from the hallway. The thought was frightening. Where had they gone? Were they plotting an attack? Brandy had lost her candle during the 'floor show', but they were able to see enough of the creepy corridor to find the study entrance. They just about reached the study when the floor turned to sand, and Eva fell through, losing her sword across the floor. Eva cried out while grasping at the floor surrounding her that seemed to crumble in her hands.

Brandy leapt to the floor, braced her feet on either side of the stable portion of the opening, and attempted to keep Eva from falling through. Eva clung to Brandy's wrists while trying to catch onto something, anything, with her feet. Dirty, decayed hands clutched Eva's feet and legs from the depths of the darkness below and attempted to pull her down with them. Eva screamed hysterically while kicking at the hands clutching at her legs. Brandy slid closer to the opening, losing her grip on Eva's wrists as the creatures below pulled on her friend. A hand suddenly appeared from behind Brandy. She jumped with a startled scream and saw Raven grab Eva's arm. With little effort, he heaved her from the pit. The floor immediately closed, attempting to ensnare Eva, but she was already free. Eva jumped back a step as she looked at the now solid floor while gasping for her breath. Brandy jumped from the floor and into Raven's arms.

"We thought you were dead," Brandy gasped while clinging to him.

Raven briefly returned the embrace, kissing her forehead before pulling away and scanning the corridor.

"It'll take more than a cheap haunting to stop me," Raven scoffed, seeming almost angry about what happened. "Where are the others?"

"Gone," Brandy gasped. "That *thing* got them."

Eva reclaimed her sword, looking more determined now and possibly a little pissed. Raven hurried both women into the study to regroup and strategize their next move.

Chapter 33

Once they entered the study, Eva slammed and locked the door behind them while Brandy rushed to the desk and pulled out the drawers, casting them onto the floor, leaving Raven slightly bewildered.

"There may be an answer to all of this in my father's journal," Brandy informed Raven. "We need to find it."

Eva ran to the shelves and began tearing books from them, haphazardly casting them onto the floor. Raven approached Brandy and placed a black leather book on the desk. She looked at the journal, then lifted her head and met his gaze. His almost emotionless expression frightened her. Brandy stared at him, confused.

"Where'd you get this?" Brandy asked, now concerned.

Eva stopped rummaging through the bookcase and uncertainly approached Raven from behind while gripping her sword with distrust in her eyes.

"I had it the entire time," Raven informed her.

Brandy and Eva's expressions dropped to near horror at the confession. Eva raised her sword, prepared to strike him down at a moment's notice. With his back still turned to her, Raven raised his finger to Eva, warning her against whatever she had in mind. Eva held her ground but didn't make any sudden moves.

"I came for it as soon as I'd heard the news about Cullen's death," Raven informed her.

"Why?" Brandy asked before her eyes suddenly widened as she gasped in horror. "You're my half-brother?"

Raven immediately grimaced and shook his head. "My God, no!" he cried out, then tensed. "Your father and I were best friends. I was concerned your brother might come after you when he learned about your inheritance. I thought it might be best if I kept an eye on you and his journal."

Brandy suddenly gasped with realization, "Nevar!"

"Yes, I'm Nevar. Raven is an antigram," he informed her. "Your father gave me that nickname when I was a rowdy teenager, and it kind of stuck."

"So you knew the entire time that this house was haunted?" Brandy demanded, feeling her anger with Raven increasing.

"This house isn't haunted," Raven insisted. "It never was." He frowned and shook his head. "It's cursed."

Eva appeared even more concerned while keeping her sword close, although still untrusting.

"Cursed? Cursed by what?" Eva demanded, frightened.

"Not by what," Raven remarked. "By whom. Cursed by Brandy's warlock brother, Ford. He wants the journal."

"He can have it!" Brandy cried out.

Eva appeared shocked and slowly lowered the sword. "Wait, back it up," she remarked. "Did you just say *warlock* brother?"

Brandy now realized what he'd said as well. "Warlock?" she gasped.

Raven briefly glanced at Eva. "Yes, I said warlock," he remarked, then looked at Brandy. "Your father was a powerful warlock."

"So you're saying Brandy is a witch?" Eva gasped, her eyes widening.

"Of course I'm not," Brandy scoffed. "That's ridiculous."

"I know it's difficult to accept, Brandy, but you are a half witch," Raven informed her.

Brandy allowed her head to fall into her hands as she groaned lowly. "Great," she muttered. "Just what I needed today."

"Does that mean she can cast spells and do magic?" Eva asked, almost enthusiastically.

Brandy lifted her head and glared at Eva with annoyance. "Don't be ridiculous!"

"She's absolutely right," Raven announced and nodded. "You've always had the powers. You just haven't consciously used them because you didn't know they'd existed. Once you accept your birthright, you'll find your powers."

"I don't care about any of this," Brandy launched hotly. "I just want to escape this nightmare!" She then hesitated and eyed him almost suspiciously. "Wait. How do you know so much about this?"

Eva's eyes suddenly widened as she pointed her sword at him, her face filled with horror at the realization. "He's one of them," she cried out. "He's a fucking warlock!"

Brandy stared at Raven with horror. "Is Eva right?" she gasped. "Are you a warlock?"

Raven slowly nodded.

"Can you stop this?" Eva eagerly asked.

"I'm afraid I can't," Raven informed her. "At the moment, I'm stuck in this curse with you. I have no way of reversing it or escaping it."

"So you knew what was going on the entire time, yet you allowed me to think I was insane?" Brandy suddenly demanded, becoming angry at him all over again.

"No, that's not the case," Raven replied, defensively. "I've been looking for Ford since I arrived, but I couldn't find anything to indicate he was actually here."

"I told you the place was haunted," Brandy reminded him with increasing hostility. "Why didn't you put it together? You should've known."

"Everything you'd described to me in the beginning sounded like little more than a young witch coming to terms with her powers," Raven informed her. "Being in your father's house triggered what was inside you, setting it free. It's why he left you the house in the first place." He hesitated as he studied her confused and concerned expression. "You may not want to believe it, but I'm convinced that incident with the statue was all you."

"Me? I did that?" Brandy suddenly gasped, then hesitated and nervously looked around. "But you're sure he's here now? I mean, I'm not doing all this, am I?"

"No," Raven replied. "What I've seen tonight is more elaborate than a beginner witch could conjure."

"So why don't we just give Ford the journal, if it's what he wants?" Eva asked.

"Cullen's journal contains his most powerful spells," Raven replied. "Ford can't get his hands on it. But it's not just the journal he wants. He wants the house and revenge."

"Revenge? On whom?" Brandy demanded.

"You, I'm afraid," Raven replied. "He's insane. You can give him everything he wants, and he's still going to make you suffer."

"So how do we get away?" Eva asked.

"We're stuck," Raven informed her while shrugging. "The only way to end this would be for him to stop it on his own or if we were to find a way to defeat him."

"So he's just toying with us," Brandy huffed, defeated. "He could kill us at any time. We can't beat him."

Eva raised her sword with a stern look. "I say we kill the bastard."

"It's not as easy as that," Raven reminded her. "However, what he's doing requires a great deal of power and concentration. He can't keep up this elaborate show for very long. In a fair fight, he's no match for me, so he must've known I would show up."

"So Jana knew you were my father's friend?" Brandy asked.

"No," Raven replied. "She never saw me when I visited your father. I'd only ever met him in the cigar lounge in the evenings when she and Parker were around. She and Parker never knew Cullen was a warlock." Raven then cocked his head. "And, no, your father wasn't *fraternizing* with Jana. He wasn't home a lot the last couple of years and basically wanted someone who wouldn't ask too many questions."

"I can see why he might want someone like Jana then," Brandy remarked. "What do we do about Ford?"

"If I can find him, I can beat him," Raven informed her, then considered their situation. "In forty-eight hours, if I don't contact Rockwell, he'll be showing up with a few of our warlock friends."

"Attorney Rockwell?" Brandy gasped, surprised. "He's a warlock too?"

"Of course he is," Raven replied. "We're a pretty tight-knit community. We prearranged it just in case something like this happened. It would be impossible for Ford to fight more than one warlock."

"I don't think it'll matter much in forty-eight hours," Eva remarked. "We're not going to last that long."

"So what do we do now?" Brandy asked Raven.

"You're safe as long as you're with me," Raven informed them. "He'll wear himself down in a few hours, then we can attempt to leave."

"I say we hunt him down and burn him at the stake!" Eva cried out.

Raven gave Eva an icy stare. "I find that particularly offensive."

Eva appeared embarrassed and grimaced. "Sorry, I forgot."

"Stay alert, because he'll be coming after you next, Eva," Raven informed her. "And that sword isn't going to protect you any more than harsh language. Warlocks can't be killed that easily."

"If you can defeat him, then that's what we should do," Eva announced, again invigorated. "Let's find the bastard!"

Raven stared at Eva with some surprise, then looked at Brandy. She shrugged and attempted a tiny smile.

"I hate to admit it, but I'm with Eva," Brandy remarked. "If you can defeat him, why play on his terms?"

Raven groaned and shook his head. "You're both insane," he informed them. "It's pretty simple. If I'm focused on hunting him, I can't ensure your safety. One thing at a time."

"He took our friends," Brandy reminded Raven. "We want him to pay. It's a risk we're willing to take. You worry about defeating him, Eva and I will watch our own backs."

Raven groaned softly as he replaced the journal inside his jacket, where it instantly disappeared, surprising the women, then motioned them to the study door.

"If you really want to do this," Raven announced. "I have a pretty good idea where to start looking."

Chapter 34

Brandy and Eva followed Raven into the grand hallway, where both women stopped and watched the white knight's horse trot down the hall past them. It felt as if they were the first ones up at some wild frat party. Paula suddenly screamed somewhere within the house, causing both women to jump.

"Paula," Brandy gasped.

"It's a trick," Raven informed them. "He's trying to provoke you into making snap decisions and fall into some elaborate trap."

"Is she alive?" Brandy asked.

"Right now, your friends are worth more to him alive. He needs them as leverage over you," Raven informed her. "We'll start in the basement. More than likely, that's where we'll find him and your friends."

"The basement," Eva cried out, now paranoid. "That *thing* is down there!"

"That *thing* is gone," Raven assured them.

Brandy suddenly looked at him with surprise. "That wolf was you, wasn't it?"

"We can take on many forms," Raven informed her, then shrugged. "That particular occasion called for teeth."

"I bet you're a lot of fun at parties," Eva remarked, slightly humored.

Raven glared at Eva, who met his stern gaze and chuckled at his expense.

"But we were in the basement," Brandy reminded him. "We didn't see anyone down there."

"Now, you're in my world," he informed her. "Things aren't always what they seem. Just because you didn't see your friends, that doesn't mean they weren't there."

§

As they stepped into the basement corridor, thick fog rolled along the stone floor, horrifying Eva and Brandy. Raven walked through the fog without a second thought.

"Fog," Eva whispered, chilled at the sight of the substance covering the floor.

"I've got a bad feeling about this, Raven," Brandy remarked.

"This?" Raven asked, then kicked the fog with disgust. "This is just a cheap warlock trick. No imagination. Come on."

"We've seen what that cheap trick can do to a person," Eva informed him.

"It turned Jana to ice," Brandy remarked.

"I learned that trick in warlock preschool," Raven muttered. "Don't be too quick to believe what you think you've seen."

Brandy and Eva uncertainly followed him through the fog, not nearly as convinced. Something moved stealthily beneath the fog behind Eva and Brandy, following them. They could hear a woman crying from within one of the cells. Raven hurried to one of the end cells as the mass within the fog continued to glide behind the unsuspecting women. Raven opened the cell door and found Jana sitting in the corner of the empty chamber. She was wet, naked, and shivering. Raven hurried into the cell.

"Jana, are you all right?" Raven asked.

Jana clung to her knees and shivered. "So cold--" she whispered.

Raven removed his jacket and placed it over her shoulders. Once she slipped into the jacket, he helped her to her feet. Brandy and Eva remained within the corridor and stared at the shivering maid with ice in her hair. Eva suddenly let out a startled cry, alarming Brandy. She then jumped and stared at the fog on the floor.

"Something moved past my legs," Eva cried out.

Brandy looked nervously around the fog as Raven entered the hall with his arm around the shivering maid.

"We need to get her upstairs and warm her up," Raven announced. "She's in shock."

Something snake-like suddenly moved beneath the fog near them. Jana screamed hysterically while clutching Raven's arm. A ghostly snake figure, formed from the fog, rose before Eva. It hissed with large fangs, and its long tail attempted to wrap itself around her. Eva screamed and slashed at the fog with her sword. The fog snake vanished as the sword sliced through it. Jana's face remained buried into Raven's shoulder while she continued screaming. After conquering the fog snake, Eva's look was serious and more determined. She then looked at Raven with a sly grin and twirled the sword.

"If you think that was impressive," Eva announced, "wait until I start cursing."

§

Brandy and Eva sat on the bed in Jana's room while staring at the bathroom door. There was a thump from within the bathroom right before Raven entered the bedroom with his jacket. As he wiped water from his face, both women stared at him.

"Well, she's back to her usual, annoying self," Raven scoffed.

"What happened?" Brandy asked.

"She wanted me to join her," Raven replied.

"Apparently, she's not too distraught over her ordeal," Eva remarked, then sighed and stood. "I'll keep an eye on her."

"Be my guest," Raven muttered.

Eva entered the bathroom and shut the door behind her while Raven collapsed on the bed near Brandy. Brandy studied his profile a moment, feeling a little conflicted. The man sitting alongside her wasn't just *who* he said he was, but he wasn't even *what* she thought he was. Of course, according to him, she wasn't *what* she thought she was either. It was the first time she had a moment to actually think about who and what Raven really was. She wasn't sure if his being a warlock terrified her or excited her. Brandy pushed her thoughts on Raven aside and returned to the more pressing issue.

"We have to find my friends, Raven," Brandy insisted. "They're somewhere within this house. I can hear their screams."

"They're here all right," Raven informed her. "But I doubt it's them you're hearing. Your brother is playing on your feelings for your friends. He's going to use your emotions to trick you." He then hesitated and appeared to sink into thought. "They're in the house, but he must have them hidden in an alternate dimension."

"An alternate dimension," Brandy gasped, alarmed at the thought. "How will we ever find them?"

"Finding his manufactured dimension won't be nearly as difficult as you think," Raven insisted. "We just need to find the doorway. It's probably been staring us in the face the entire time, but we just didn't notice it. He's wasting a lot of magic to keep up this hoax *and* retain an alternate dimension."

Brandy considered his words, but her mind kept straying back to Raven being a warlock as well as her father's best friend. She stared at him for a long moment before finally looking down.

"So you knew my father well?" she asked almost timidly.

"We were friends for a very long time," Raven replied.

She looked up and met his gaze with a serious look. "Why didn't he want to see me?"

"It's not that he didn't want to see you, Brandy," Raven informed her somewhat delicately. "He had to send you and your mother away after an incident involving Ford's mother." He drew a deep breath, then released it. "A few years before your parents met, Ford's mother placed a spell on your father, seducing him. He was a powerful warlock and would produce a powerful offspring."

Brandy stared at him, horrified. "You can do that?" she gasped, now concerned about what she'd been feeling for the man she thought was her butler. "Manipulate affections?"

"It's nearly impossible to accomplish," Raven insisted, then appeared to read her mind. "And not a spell a warlock could ever perform on a witch, in case you were wondering."

"Never crossed my mind," Brandy remarked, although he knew she was lying.

"The council found out and banished her for her actions. It's a serious crime in our society. When Ford's mother discovered your father's relationship with Nadia, she threatened to kill her out of jealousy.

His mother was an evil, insane witch, and Cullen was afraid she'd hurt both of you, so he had to keep you a secret from her. That meant he'd have to stay away until he was sure she wouldn't come back."

"How long did he intend to wait?" Brandy asked, her irritation returning.

"About five years ago, Ford's mother was cast to stone for further infractions against our society," Raven informed her. "Cullen was finally free from her threats. It was around that time that your mother started dating a man named Gilford." He stared into her eyes, seeming hesitant to continue. "Gilford is Cullen. He's your father."

"Gilford is my father?" Brandy gasped, shocked by his words.

"He was finally able to return, but he didn't know how you'd react," Raven replied. "He always loved you and your mother, and they intended to tell you everything when the time was right." Raven seemed hesitant. "Your mother knew why Gilford didn't return from his 'business trip'. A few weeks before his death, Ford confronted your father and made some pretty serious threats. Confident he didn't know anything about you or your mother, Cullen decided to go away for a few weeks, in case Ford tried something. Apparently, he did."

Brandy allowed her head to fall into her hands with a saddened look. "This is horrible. My poor mother," she gasped. "Gilford? I can't believe it. All these years." Brandy shook her head, then finally looked back at Raven. "He should have told me."

"I know he should have, but he couldn't bring himself to do it," Raven informed her. "He knew it'd cause problems for a while, and he didn't want to chance losing you again. He liked his relationship with you as it was."

"I guess I was wrong about him all these years. He stayed away because he loved me, not because he didn't want me," Brandy remarked and again looked at Raven. "Thank you, Raven." Brandy placed her hand on his. "It was very thoughtful of you to come out here and look after me."

Raven clutched her hand and smiled warmly. "It was the least I could do for Cullen. After all we'd been through," he replied.

Brandy smiled and laughed softly. She looked down a moment in silence, then glanced at Raven and smiled gently.

"I don't really know what's real and what's not anymore," Brandy remarked timidly. "I mean, what we discussed about relationships. Was that real? You aren't married, are you? To a witch, perhaps."

Raven continued to stroke her hand and laughed softly. "No," he replied gently. "Everything I told you was the truth. Warlocks have a tough time finding women who can tolerate them. Most witches don't like warlocks, and mortal women can't cope with our attitudes. We mature incredibly slowly." He smiled weakly. "I'm seventy-six, and I only matured a year or so ago."

"Seventy-six?"

"We live a very long time," Raven informed her. "The same goes for half-witches."

"No girlfriend either?" she asked.

"Actually," he announced. "I kind of had my eye on my best friend's daughter." A smile crossed his face. "Cullen thought we'd be good together."

"He did, did he?" she asked, then smiled with some embarrassment.

"I took an interest in you several years ago, but Cullen insisted I stay away until I matured," Raven informed her. "As I said, we mature slowly. By the time he felt I was mature enough, Ford was causing drama. He had to disappear for a while, and I was keeping an eye on you and your mother."

"You were?"

"Unconventional methods," Raven replied while offering a tiny smile. "Stray cats, birds in the parks. Not in a creepy way. Just trying to keep you safe."

"That was you," she remarked. "The cat in my apartment." She became somewhat concerned. "You were in my bedroom that night."

Raven eyed her with some surprise. "I *was* the cat in your apartment, but I wasn't in your bedroom," he insisted. "I wouldn't have done that."

"So that was him?" Brandy gasped, alarmed. "That was Ford?"

Raven frowned and nodded. "I assume so."

"Attorney Rockwell never called the agency, did he?" she asked. "That was all you."

"Actually, Rockwell told me you were reacting strangely to his presence," Raven informed her. "It's not uncommon for young witches, unaware of their lineage, to have their powers manifest spontaneously in the presence of witch society elders."

"He's high up in your society?" she asked, then shook her head. "I knew something felt 'off' when he got too close to me."

Raven nodded, knowingly. "Because of that, we both felt you needed a little supervision. It's possible his mere presence heightened your 'witchy senses', for lack of a better term. If your powers were awakened without you knowing who and what you were, it could cause all sorts of trouble. Some of which we saw in the garden that first night." He stared into her eyes for a long moment. "When I helped cure your headache, with a little warlock voodoo, I was hoping to calm you as well. Instead, you enchanted me with your own spell." He hid his smile. "And although I kind of enjoyed it, I knew better than to act upon it."

"That wasn't witchcraft," Brandy informed him. "That was just good old-fashioned seduction. Don't blame me that you didn't act upon it."

"I'm glad you have a sense of humor about it," Raven replied with a soft chuckle. He then seemed slightly tense. "I wasn't sure how you were going to react to all of this. I'm still waiting for the part where you're repulsed because I'm a warlock and throw me to the curb."

Brandy stared at him a moment and realized her feelings hadn't changed at all. She gently touched his face while staring into his eyes.

"That's not happening," she insisted. "I'm not repulsed that you're a warlock. Quite the opposite. And when this is all over, I hope we can continue seeing each other." She hesitated a moment, then grinned slyly. "Preferably in the shower."

Raven groaned softly and pulled her into his arms. "I'd like that," he announced, then kissed her warmly.

Chapter 35

Eva sat on the sink within the bathroom while Jana soaked in the tub, talking to her from the other side of the shower curtain. Water from within the tub gently splashed as Eva watched Jana's silhouette.

"It was pretty frightening to wake up in that cell," Jana remarked almost timidly. "I felt like I'd been in a freezer."

"We really thought you'd been killed," Eva informed her. "Seeing you turned to ice then shattering like that."

"In the dungeon, there were all these spiders," Jana remarked, then shivered.

Eva groaned. "I know that feeling."

"You've been so kind to me, Eva," Jana insisted. "I wish there were something I could do for you."

"You could get me out of this house of fun," Eva huffed.

"You know, I think I know a way."

Eva stood and approached the curtain. "You do? What's your idea?"

The curtain was suddenly torn open from the opposite side, revealing the mermaid within the tub in

Jana's place. Eva gasped and jumped back, but not fast enough. The mermaid's tongue shot out, grabbed Eva around her arm and shoulder, and pulled her over the side of the tub into the water. Eva screamed as she splashed within the water of the tub that seemed much wider now, while fighting the massive tongue wrapped around her, attempting to pull her into the mermaid's mouth. All Eva saw was massive rows of teeth as she was pulled beneath the surface, the water muffling her screams. Eva surfaced from the depths of the tub, clinging to the side with a gasp and a scream. Raven and Brandy were heard pounding on the bathroom door from the other side, attempting to get to her. The mermaid looked more like an eel now, wrapped around Eva. As it disappeared under the water, Eva's legs kicked at the creature, attempting to break free.

"Help!"

The eel wrapped around her legs as well as the rest of her body as she was submerged under the water, struggling to keep the fanged mouth away from her face. The bathroom door was thrown open with a loud crack, splintering the doorframe, revealing Raven. Brandy attempted to run past him into the bathroom, but he entered first, keeping her behind him. The shower curtain was now closed, and they didn't hear any sounds coming from the tub. Raven approached the bathtub and yanked open the curtain. The tub was now filled with blood, but there was no sign of Eva or Jana.

"Eva!" Brandy cried out.

Raven grabbed her arm to keep her from getting closer to the tub. "Don't believe everything you see," he informed her. "Come on!"

Despite her attempt to run to the bathtub, Raven pulled Brandy from the bathroom.

Raven and Brandy hurried along the first floor hallway while Brandy was nearly hysterical over her missing friend, looking at Raven every few feet.

"We have to find her," Brandy cried out. "She's not dead. She's here somewhere."

"I agree, but I don't know where to look," Raven insisted.

Brandy suddenly stopped him, realization on her face. "I think I do."

They heard a horse's loud squeal. Both looked at the foyer doors and saw the black knight sitting on his horse, blocking the doorway. The horse suddenly reared, and the knight charged at them. Raven threw Brandy into the library and out of the path of the approaching knight. He cast his hand forward, and the black horse vanished when it touched his hand. The knight crashed to the hall floor with a loud clatter of his armor, but quickly returned to a standing position with his sword drawn. Raven was slightly surprised by the knight's fast recovery. When the knight swung his sword, Raven ducked the blade and dove into the library with Brandy. Raven slammed the door behind him and braced the door with his body while panting. Brandy stared at him, not sure what to say after what she'd seen.

"That rotten bastard!" Raven snarled, his hostility increasing.

The tip of the broadsword suddenly erupted through Raven's chest, having penetrated the door behind him. He cried out with surprise and agony while looking at the sword exposed from his chest. Brandy screamed and ran to him as the sword was roughly pulled back out through the door. Raven fell to his knees while clutching his bleeding chest, looking more surprised than anything.

"Raven! No!"

Raven suddenly burst into flames while Brandy fell backward and stared at his burning body in horror. He almost immediately incinerated and turned to smoke. Brandy jumped to her feet with a look of shock. She suddenly screamed long and loud as her fear turned to anger.

"No!"

The windows and glass doors violently shattered from her emotional scream. Wind suddenly whipped through the room while Brandy stood motionless with hatred in her eyes. She shot a look at the library door, and it was ripped off its hinges and then flew across the room. An enraged Brandy slowly and boldly walked through the open doorway into the hall with the wind blowing past her. She stared down the long hallway as the ballroom doors slammed behind the black knight on his horse. The wind harshly whipped past her, striking the ballroom doors, and they flew open with a thunderous bang. With a look of hatred and determination, Brandy ran down the hall to the ballroom, picking up speed as she reached the double doors. As she entered the ballroom at top speed, she saw the black knight on his horse just ahead as he galloped for the painting. The horse jumped through the canvas, vanishing inside it. Brandy continued running across the ballroom for the large painting of the castle and countryside in the distance. As she dove headfirst for the painting, she transformed into a black panther while leaping through it.

Chapter 36

Within the English countryside, inside the painting, the black panther leapt on top of the knight and knocked him from his horse. He immediately turned to dust upon impact, leaving only an armor shell. Brandy returned to her human form and leapt onto the horse's back. She sent the horse into a gallop across the countryside toward the distant castle. Somehow, it was the same mansion but looking more like a castle with tall turrets, and a drawbridge over an actual moat. She rode the horse across the medieval drawbridge, its hooves thundering across the thick wood, and entered the courtyard. She abruptly stopped the horse and looked around the quiet courtyard. She eyed the castle walls and the tower high above. Stone gargoyles were perched every twenty feet along the castle wall, seemingly watching her. The stone cracked by their clawed feet, and she heard a soft growl. Brandy saw the small stone chips fall into the courtyard and looked up again.

At least ten stone gargoyles flew from their perches on enormous wings and buzzed down toward her. She cried out and jumped off the horse. The horse snorted, spun, and ran away. As Brandy flipped onto her backside, a stone gargoyle flew straight for her. She rolled out of its path, sprang to her feet, and ran to the castle door with the stone gargoyle directly on her heels. She entered the castle and slammed the door behind her. The stone gargoyle struck the door and crumbled. Brandy leaned against the heavy door for a moment while attempting to catch her breath. She looked around the familiar yet somehow unfamiliar foyer and staircase. The grand staircase seemed taller and longer now with stone steps, while the railing pillars had stone dragons that were now moving, flapping their large wings, almost daring her to pass. The small landing still boasted the large stained glass window, but there were no jousting knights or the castle. She'd found the alternate dimension Raven had told her about.

When she heard Eva screaming from upstairs, Brandy ran for the familiar staircase. Dirty and decrepit hands exploded from the floor, grabbing her ankles and dragging her to the floor. Brandy fought them, kicking and punching them. More hands appeared and captured her arms and shoulders while she screamed. She was suddenly pulled beneath the hall floor, falling quite a distance before roughly landing in a dungeon cell with a thud. She pulled herself to her feet and looked around the dim chamber, now trapped. Brandy ran to the cell door and pulled on it, but it was locked. She took a step back and glared at the door. It pinged and flew open. Brandy hurried from the cell and into the corridor now lit by torches. A human-like creature without skin approached her from the stairs while carrying a sword. It began running toward her and raised its weapon. She then heard a growling sound behind her. Brandy half-turned and saw a similar creature approaching from the opposite direction.

Brandy eyed both. When they were almost upon her, she jumped back into the cell, allowing one to stab the other accidentally. Brandy jumped into the corridor, rolled across the floor, snatched the discarded sword, maneuvered to one knee, and blocked the creature's weapon. When the creature pulled back to strike again, Brandy swung at its knees, slicing through them. The beast fell with a squeal, shattering into a hundred snakes, and slithered toward her.

"Cheap warlock trick," she scoffed in anger.

Brandy grabbed a torch from the wall and waved it at the snakes. They steamed, dehydrated, and turned to dust. Brandy carried the torch and the sword as she cautiously climbed the stone steps. The narrow stone staircase wound several times as the torch created its own shadows. A shadow moved behind her, taking on a human form. Arms lifted to reveal shadow claws towering over her. Brandy stopped and whirled around to see the shadow about to strike. Her eyes narrowed as she casually tossed the torch down the steps. The shadow was sucked down the stairs with the light. Brandy smiled and snorted a laugh. She then turned and continued up the stairs.

Chapter 37

Brandy again entered the first floor corridor with the sword clutched in her hands. She was now more determined than ever to defeat her brother's little house of horror. The grand hallway seemed longer and broader than it had in her dimension. The old slate floor no longer had any throw rugs, but the walls were adorned with tapestries. The tall, exposed-beam ceiling had chandeliers lit by thick candles rather than electricity. Oddly enough, the furniture was exactly the same, but the suits of armor posted alongside each of the eight doorways were actual knights and not empty armor. Each turned their head and watched her, possibly waiting to strike. Brandy could hear Eva scream from somewhere upstairs. As she stared at the ceiling, she stood frozen for a moment, debating her next move. Eva's screams were being used to get a knee-jerk reaction from her. Ford wanted her to make snap decisions based on emotion, but she wasn't falling for it.

Brandy walked cautiously down the hallway and looked into several rooms as she passed while also keeping an eye on each knight. When she heard beastly snarls, she stopped before the dining room and looked inside. The dining room looked almost exactly as it had, but with more tapestries on the walls. Beastly human, wild boar hybrids with large eyes, long snouts, and fangs sat around the thick table, slopping down piles of human innards like pigs at a trough. Brandy was, for the first time, momentarily horrified. She was in a nightmare of her half-brother's making. Since his decayed human-like creatures didn't rattle her, had Ford upped the ante? Brandy slipped past the dining room and looked across the hall to the library. On the library floor, she saw Raven motionless with blood covering his chest.

Brandy withheld her gasp while running to the library doorway. She stopped just short of the doorway and clutched the frame while holding her breath, staring at Raven's dead, motionless body. She buried her emotions deep inside. It was a trick! She was almost positive Ford was just trying to unhinge her. Raven wasn't dead. She refused to believe he was dead any more than she believed her friends were dead. Brandy gathered her strength, turned away from the library, and hurried along the hallway past the other rooms without looking into any of them. Despite hearing things in the nearby rooms, she knew it was all a distraction. She approached the grand staircase and swung the banister about to head up the steps when she heard a familiar voice.

"Brandy!" Raven called to her.

Brandy suddenly stopped and looked back. Raven slowly stumbled along the hallway while clutching his bleeding chest. Brandy took two steps toward him and once more stopped. Raven was weak and could barely walk.

"Brandy, thank God you're here," Raven announced as he made his way closer. "I thought I'd lost you."

Brandy took two quick steps toward him, raised the sword to his throat, and squinted at him. "I'm not *that* stupid."

Raven suddenly pushed the sword away and tossed her to the floor while transforming into a skinless, rotted creature.

"I think you are," the familiar evil voice hissed as the creature hovered over her.

Brandy screamed, momentarily horrified, before her anger resurfaced and she suddenly transformed into a black panther. She leaped for the creature and tackled it to the floor, clinging to it with her long claws, and tore into its neck with her teeth, while violently digging her back claws into its mid-section. Her claws ripped the rotted flesh from its body, spattering thick, goopy blood. The creature suddenly fell apart and collapsed to the floor. Brandy returned to her human form and scrambled to her feet while reclaiming her sword. She stared at the chunks of rotted flesh littered along the floor. The flesh turned into fat, hairy spiders and scattered in every direction. Brandy couldn't help but scream. Trick or not, she hated spiders! She clutched her sword, spun, and ran up the stairs. As Brandy neared the landing, she heard a loud creak.

When she stopped and looked up, Eva suddenly plummeted downward with a hangman's noose around her neck. She came to an abrupt halt just before the stained-glass window, and her neck snapped with a loud, hideous crack. Eva's body twitched a moment, then gently swayed. Anger now consumed Brandy. She screamed in rage and frustration while coiling back with the sword and violently cast it into the stained-glass window. When the window shattered, air was sucked from the room like a vacuum, taking Eva's body out the window. Several paintings, vases, and other small objects followed. Brandy clung to the railing to keep from being sucked up in the vacuum until she reached the second set of stairs past the landing, no longer feeling the force of the wind. Brandy rushed up the stairs to the left and paused at the beginning of the second floor corridor. What was being thrown at her was straight out of her worst nightmares. There were long, deep scratches in the walls, oozing blood, and every shut door seemed to breathe, bulging in and out, with faint moans coming from each of the rooms.

Brandy had to admit, as Ford upped the game, she was becoming increasingly unnerved, but she couldn't let his cheap warlock tricks stop her. At least, she hoped they were cheap warlock tricks. Brandy hurried down the corridor, ignoring the bulging doors, and finally reached the master bedroom. Without barely stopping, Brandy threw her hand in the direction of the door, and it violently flew open with a crash. The master bedroom looked almost the same, with the familiar large, heavy Victorian furniture and the tall, king-sized hardtop canopy bed, but with heavy bed curtains on all sides. Brandy entered the medieval chamber and immediately saw Eva chained by her wrist and clinging to the bedpost, wearing a medieval queen's dress.

"Behind you," Eva shouted.

Brandy spun around as the door slammed shut. A frightened Jana, still in her clothing from earlier that night, stood near the closed door.

"Don't trust her," Jana screamed. "That's not Eva, it's Ford! He's trying to trick you!"

"It's a trick, Brandy," Eva shouted. "Jana's your brother's girlfriend!"

"He killed Eva," Jana cried out in panic. "I saw him hang her from the rafters! You have to destroy him now!"

"She's lying," Eva shouted back. "It's really me, Brandy! Ask me anything!"

"There's no time to lose," Jana cried out. "Raven's not dead yet. We can still save him. Ford turned him into a stone statue in the garden!"

Brandy appeared undecided, looking back and forth between the two women.

Eva turned furious and screamed, "Get me out of this fucking dress!"

Brandy suddenly spun toward Jana and threw a fireball at her. Jana screamed and instantly turned into a vapor. Her screams were heard within the vapor as it seeped from the room. Eva clung to the bedpost and sighed with relief.

"I was scared you were going to believe her for a minute there," Eva groaned.

Brandy snorted a slightly uneasy laugh. "When I saw you in that dress, I almost believed her," she remarked and held her hand over the shackle, popping it open. "Only the real Eva knows she wouldn't be caught dead in a dress."

Eva pulled her hand free, gingerly rubbed her wrist, and then eyed the open shackle before looking back at Brandy.

"Uh, how did you do that?" Eva asked.

"We can talk about that another time," Brandy informed her.

"We have to get out of here," Eva insisted. "He's here *somewhere*." She then looked around and grimaced. "But where the hell is *here*?"

"We're in another dimension hidden inside the ballroom painting," Brandy informed her. "Our friends have to be here somewhere. They're not dead. Raven's not dead. I'm positive of it."

"He got Raven?" Eva suddenly grabbed Brandy's arm with a look of fear in her eyes. "If Raven couldn't stop him, how can we?"

"It's all we've got, Eva," Brandy informed her. "You have to believe we can."

Eva held her breath and then nodded, appearing more determined. "Let's catch us a warlock," she announced.

Chapter 38

Fog rolled along the stone dungeon corridor and into the torture chamber, where it rose and rapidly took a human form. Jana appeared within the fog with an enraged look upon her face. There was a faint clunk behind her. She suddenly turned, looked around the room, and gasped before smiling nervously.

"Ford, stop appearing like that," Jana scoffed. "You know it unnerves me."

Dexter, Eva's ex-boyfriend, lay casually on the stretching rack facing her, wearing an evil, twisted smile on his face. He sprang to his feet and approached her.

"You seem to have forgotten the real reason behind being here, Jana," Dexter reminded her.

"No, Ford, I haven't," she insisted while sulking. "I've looked for that journal day and night since Cullen's been gone." She shook her head, almost defeated. "If Raven has it, he didn't bring it with him. I'd even searched his room. It's not as if I could catch him off guard, either. He's far too stubborn. I wasn't prepared to have Cullen's warlock buddies showing up."

"He's not stubborn, he's acting upon instinct," Dexter informed her. "He's too clever for you. I'll find the journal; that's just a matter of time." He turned angry while glaring at her. "It was your job to confuse Brandy and keep her frightened. She wasn't allowed to regain control."

"Raven alerted her to her powers," Jana informed him. "How am I supposed to fight that? You have to give me more power."

"I've given you far too much power already," Dexter snarled while pausing before her and glaring into her eyes. "I gave you the power to create your own magic to frighten Brandy. And what did you do with it?" His eyes narrowed. "You used it to free Eva from her stone casing so you could torture her!"

"I wouldn't do that," Jana announced, now defensive and possibly a little frightened. "I don't know how she got free."

"Liar!"

When Dexter pointed his finger at her, a gust of wind pushed her slowly backward toward the spiked Iron Maiden. Jana struggled to keep from sliding backward.

"Stop! You're scaring me!"

"You're jealous of Eva," Dexter scoffed. "You were afraid I actually had feelings for her, and you intended to harm her so that I wouldn't want her!"

"No, that's not true! I wouldn't cross you!" Jana cried out while fighting his power over her.

"You're right, because you'll never have another chance," Dexter snarled, then flicked his fingers at her.

Jana was violently thrown backward against the spikes in the back of the Iron Maiden. She gasped with wide, horror-filled eyes, blood seeping from her mouth. The doors slammed shut, followed by a muffled grunt. Only a moment later, blood trickled from the bottom of the Iron Maiden.

§

The medieval master bedroom began to vibrate as if an earthquake had struck. Brandy and Eva looked around, horrified, and grabbed onto the thick bedposts to keep their balance. The floor cracked, and blood erupted like a small volcano. Both women screamed as the floor was quickly flooded with blood. When something rippled through the blood, Brandy and Eva gasped and jumped onto the bed, grabbing their respective bedpost. Zombie alligators leapt from the blood and snapped at them. As the two women clung to their bedposts, the bed began to buck, and the blood level rose, filling the room with the dark substance, now halfway up the tall bed. The three zombie alligators attempted to climb up the foot end of the vibrating bed for them.

"Brandy," Eva cried out. "Do something!"

As the bed started to float around the room in the sea of blood, Brandy looked around, uncertain what she could do to make it stop.

"If you have any suggestions, I'm listening," Brandy shouted back.

As the bed circled the room, they saw a whirlpool forming in the center. The alligators were yanked off the bed and into the churning blood, and they would soon be next.

"Brandy," Eva screamed. "Don't let me die in a dress!"

Both clung to the thick bedposts while violently being tossed in a circle around the room. Brandy then noticed that the double-glass balcony doors didn't have any blood beyond them.

"Hold on, Eva!" Brandy cried out. "I have an idea."

Eva's eyes were now wide with fear, possibly knowing what Brandy had in mind. Brandy coiled back her hand and pitched a fireball at the glass doors. As the doors exploded outward, there was an incredible rush of blood flooding toward the balcony. Every object in the room rushed out of the opening, riding on a wave of blood. Eva and Brandy screamed as the bed flew through the opening to the balcony. The bed violently struck the railing, and both women were cast from it. They clung to the thick posts to keep from falling down the waterfall of blood. The waterfall seemed to drop hundreds of feet into a river of blood below. Death seemed inevitable. The swiftly flowing blood flew over the bed and past them, drenching them in the thick, sticky substance. Eva was losing her grip on the bedpost.

"I can't hang on," Eva cried out.

Brandy looked down, struggling to hold on as well. She could make out the black marble horse statue in the garden below. Reality suddenly hit Brandy, and she looked at Eva while reaching for her.

"Take my hand," Brandy cried out.

"I can't hold on!"

"Eva, trust me!"

Eva briefly met Brandy's gaze, held her breath, and then reached out with her bloody left hand, capturing Brandy's wrist. Brandy clutched Eva's wrist as well, locking them together.

"Let go of the bed!"

"What?" Eva cried out, horrified, staring at Brandy. "Are you insane?"

"Do it!" Brandy yelled. "Now!"

They stared at each other for only a moment in a do-or-die situation. Eva closed her eyes, held her breath, and released the post. Brandy immediately released her post as well. Both women screamed as they plummeted in a freefall. Eva and Brandy fell into the garden below, landing more softly than expected. As they opened their eyes, they looked around with amazement, slowly lifting themselves and staring at the stone statues in the garden. There was no sign of the waterfall of blood, just the castle they'd fallen from. When they looked at each other, they were no longer covered in the viscous substance. Both took several steps through the garden in silence, eyeing several lifelike statues of men and women that weren't there before. As they approached, they saw that the statues were in fact their friends, turned to stone. Eva approached Jill and stared at their friend, who they thought never showed up, while Brandy paused before Raven's likeness.

"It's them," Brandy gasped. "All of our friends. He's turned them to stone."

"I don't understand," Eva remarked while shaking her head. "They weren't here before. We would have seen them."

"We're still in the alternate realm created by Ford," Brandy informed her, indicating the castle.

Further away, there was another statue. Brandy hurried across the garden and stared at her own mother, turned to stone. Alongside Nadia was Gilford, better known as Cullen, Brandy's father. It was all starting to make sense.

"How do we get out of here?" Eva asked while spinning toward her friend.

Brandy looked around, then pointed at the horse statue. "There," she announced.

"What?"

Brandy grabbed Eva's wrist and pulled her toward the statue. With some effort, Brandy climbed on and extended her hand to Eva.

"We don't have time for this," Eva insisted. "This is serious."

"I *am* being serious," Brandy retorted. "Get on!"

Once Eva had climbed onto the statue behind her friend, Brandy placed her hand on the statue's neck. The statue chipped and crumbled at the base, followed by a loud snort. The horse's head suddenly tossed upward and turned into a real horse. Brandy kicked the horse, sending it into a gallop along the garden, through the courtyard, and across the drawbridge. Eva clung to Brandy and screamed the entire way. As the countryside whizzed past on the fast and steady horse, they approached what appeared to be a mirrored image of the ballroom in front of them.

"Hold on!" Brandy cried out.

Eva saw the massive mirror in front of them, screamed, and buried her face into Brandy's back. The horse jumped high from the ground and into the mirror. Glass shattered all around them, then quickly returned to its place as they passed through. The horse landed in the ballroom, then skidded to a halt only a few feet from the painting. Eva looked down and saw that her medieval queen's dress was gone, and she was once again in the clothes she'd been wearing earlier. Brandy spun the horse around and galloped toward the glass garden doors. The doors opened as they approached, and they passed through them into the garden.

Chapter 39

Sunrise. Brandy and Eva rode the black horse into the garden as the sun was coming up. Surprisingly, the stone people were also present in their present reality. Brandy stopped the horse near Raven's statue, and both jumped off. Eva looked around, now confused.

"This can't be right," Eva remarked. "We're back where we started."

"Not exactly," Brandy informed her. "We're back in the real world and on neutral ground. We saw what Ford was hiding in his alternate dimension, which must have brought our friends back to our reality."

"What now?" Eva asked while again studying the others in statue form. "We can't simply break them out, and he's going to find us if we stay out here."

"I can't say it'll definitely work, but if we destroy Ford, we might get them back," Brandy informed Eva.

"Or he turns us to stone alongside our friends," Eva remarked. "How are we going to defeat him when Raven couldn't?"

"We'll have to wing it," Brandy replied, then looked at Eva. "Raven said Ford couldn't keep up his so-called 'haunting' for very long. He's going to be losing strength. When he does, we can go after him."

They heard a horse snorting and immediately turned toward the open ballroom doors. The black knight sat upon his horse and raised his bloodied sword before pointing it at Brandy, as if telling her she was next. Brandy sneered and shifted her eyes to the live black statue horse. The statue horse reared with a squeal, then ran for the black knight. As it reached the knight, the statue horse reared before the knight's horse, which also reared. The knight swiftly sprang from the horse and somehow landed on his feet. As the statue horse struck the knight horse, it vanished. Brandy and Eva watched as the knight briskly walked toward them on a mission while clutching his sword. Brandy stood before Eva and raised her hand. At that moment, the black knight's armor vanished, revealing Dexter.

"Interesting trick," Dexter remarked. "You learn fast."

Brandy and Eva stared at Dexter in shock.

"Dexter?" Eva gasped, horrified. "You're Brandy's half-brother?"

"I couldn't resist getting acquainted with my sister and her friends," Dexter announced, then grinned while studying Eva. "I particularly enjoyed getting to know you, Eva. Would've been more fun if Raven hadn't attacked me at the club that night. Too bad he didn't know I wasn't just stalking my half-sister, or he might have alerted you. I couldn't allow him to ruin my plans."

"Some plan," Eva scoffed. "Only a weak man seeks revenge on innocent people. Brandy's never done anything to you, and neither have I."

"That journal means a lot to me," Dexter informed Brandy. "I need it to complete my powers. Family spells are very important for gaining power." He then glared at Eva. "And there's nothing weak about making an enemy suffer. True, she never did anything to me personally, but it doesn't change the fact that my mother went insane after our father rejected her love." He again looked back at Brandy. "I wanted our father to live long enough to see you driven out of your mind. I wanted him to feel what it's like to see the one you love suffer as my mother had."

Dexter smiled as he casually leaned against Paula's statue. Brandy and Eva watched him, but remained still. Brandy wasn't sure what her chances against him were in a fair fight. She wasn't sure she was strong enough. She wasn't sure he was weak enough.

"I like them better this way," Dexter reported, then ran his hand along Paula's stone breast while offering a dirty smile.

Dexter then approached their father's statue and looked it over.

"You've never met our father, have you?" Dexter asked, then snorted a laugh. "Honestly, you're not missing much. He always was a bit of a bastard. He's more agreeable this way." He then chuckled in a sinister manner. "I would've loved to see the surprised look on his face had he known I was the one who took him down. He never would've thought I could be capable of all of this. Never in his wildest dreams."

Brandy and Eva backed up as far as the water fountain. Brandy had considered that they should make a run for it, but something inside her suddenly snapped. She glared at Dexter with anger and hatred, plotting her next move, when she heard a loud splash. Both turned as the mermaid's tongue grabbed Eva's leg and pulled it out from under her, dragging her toward the fountain. Brandy grabbed Eva's hand as she screamed and struggled to keep herself from the mermaid in the fountain. Dexter cast a fireball, hitting the mermaid and stunning her for a moment. The mermaid squealed while releasing Eva, gave Dexter a dirty look, and dove under the water.

"She's mine," Dexter snarled.

Brandy pulled Eva to her feet and attempted to conceal her behind her, but Eva was furious and unpredictable.

"Jana may object," Eva snarled.

"Hard to object when you're dead," Dexter informed her, then smiled at Raven's statue. "I suppose Raven has made me out to be the villain in this story, but I'm not. You've gotta hate him for getting involved in our *family* business."

Dexter coiled back a pitch and threw a fireball across the garden, striking Raven's stone figure. Raven's statue exploded into hundreds of pieces. Brandy gasped and ran to Raven's broken stone body, practically on her knees.

"You bastard!" Eva cried out.

Brandy touched the broken pieces while holding back her tears, then straightened and spun to see Eva now turned to stone as well. Dexter smiled deviously as he approached Eva's statue and caressed her stone face.

"Later, my love," he announced.

Brandy threw a fireball at Dexter that landed a foot before him and exploded, sending dirt flying up and into his face. Dexter wiped the dirt from his brow and glared at her, revealing a tiny smile.

"Okay, you've got my attention," Dexter announced.

As Dexter slowly walked toward her, Brandy saw Raven's stone pieces smoke and mold back together.

"I suggest we fight to the death," Dexter announced, overly confident.

When Brandy looked behind her, nothing was left of Raven. She raised her head proudly and glared at her half-brother.

"Turn them back now, or I'll destroy you," Brandy snarled.

"With what?" Dexter asked while laughing.

Brandy removed a black leather journal from her back pocket, although it hadn't been there before. It also wasn't her father's actual journal.

"With this," she announced.

Dexter's smile turned serious, and he immediately extended his hand. "Hand it over now!"

Brandy waved her hand over the journal, and it burst into flames. Dexter cried out in anger, then suddenly changed into a gray wolf and lunged for her. As he tackled Brandy to the ground, she changed into the panther and swatted him across the face. Dexter was thrown back from the powerful hit. He once again appeared human and dabbed the bleeding scratches on his face, slightly stunned. He glared at Brandy, who had also returned to her human form.

"I think I'm getting pretty good at this," Brandy announced while straightening.

Dexter's expression suddenly changed to confusion as he stared behind her. "What the--?"

"As if I'm going to fall for that," Brandy scoffed.

When she heard a loud snort behind her, Brandy suddenly spun around with a startled gasp. A giant dragon stood behind her and snorted fire from its nose, nearly hitting Dexter. Dexter jumped back and changed into a dragon as well. As the dragons collided and fought each other, Brandy dove out of their path several times. Their huge tails violently swatted each other, and they just narrowly missed the other statues. The first dragon turned into Raven, then a knight in battle armor. He swung his sword gallantly in his hand while clinging to his shield. Raven then lunged for the Dexter dragon and stabbed him in the side. Dexter roared and changed into the black knight. They began battling with swords, steel clashing and sparks flying as their swords met. They fought past several statues and moved closer to the fountain. The mermaid rose from the water and clung to the edge of the fountain, waiting for her opportunity to strike. Raven struck Dexter's sword with a powerful blow and knocked it from his hand. As Dexter changed back to his human form, he coiled back to throw a spell ball.

"Goodbye, Raven!"

The mermaid's tongue suddenly lashed out, snagged Dexter's arm, and swiftly pulled him into her mouth, completely engulfing him in one swallow. There was a flash from within the mermaid before she could dive back into the water, and she suddenly turned to stone on the side of the fountain. As Raven's armor disappeared, Brandy jumped into his arms. He held her for a long moment, then looked around. The statues slowly began to move and changed back into her friends. While Brandy's friends looked around with some confusion, Raven stared beyond them. Brandy turned and saw her father looking around, appearing disoriented. Nadia approached him with the same look of bewilderment. He hugged Nadia and then kissed her warmly. It was obvious that both were still somewhat baffled by what had happened and how they had ended up in the garden. Cullen met Brandy's gaze from across the garden and stared back at her with a surprised look before slowly approaching her.

"Brandy? What are you doing here?" Cullen asked, then looked around. "What's going on?"

When she smiled and threw her arms around him, he slowly returned the embrace.

"You don't have to pretend," Brandy gasped while holding back her tears. "I know who you really are."

"You do?" Cullen asked, then turned concerned. "I can explain--"

"Raven's already told me everything," she replied. "I understand."

Brandy then hugged her mother, relieved she was okay, especially since she didn't even realize she'd been taken in the first place. Raven stared at the mermaid statue and shook his head.

"Ford destroyed himself with his own spell," Raven informed Cullen.

"Ford?" Cullen asked while approaching Raven.

"He put a spell on you and made us think you were dead to get the journal and torture Brandy," Raven informed him.

Cullen looked at Brandy. "Oh, darling," he announced. "I'm so sorry you were put through all of this. I thought the nightmare was over after his mother's imprisonment."

"I'm just glad to have you back and to have a father finally," Brandy announced.

They again hugged. When Cullen pulled away, he looked at Raven and smiled. They exchanged a brief manly hug, then eyed Brandy's other friends, now looking disoriented.

"I think we'd better arrange a comfort spell for Brandy's friends," Cullen announced.

Raven nodded while observing the others as they milled about, appearing completely puzzled and bewildered.

"Comfort spell?" Brandy asked.

"Yeah, they'd be more comfortable not remembering what's happened," Cullen informed her.

"I see."

Eva approached with a look of concern and surprise. "You're going to wipe this from my mind?" she asked.

"It's for the best," Cullen informed her. "Our society needs to remain a secret. Besides, you've been through a major trauma."

Eva quickly looked at Brandy with sorrow and disappointment. "Brandy, don't let him erase my memory," she insisted. "I don't want to forget."

"Could you spare Eva?" Brandy asked. "She's my best friend. She can be trusted."

Cullen considered it, then eyed Raven. Raven nodded his approval of Eva. Cullen looked back at Brandy and offered a tiny smile.

"Okay," Cullen replied. "But she can't say anything *ever.*"

Eva nodded almost too enthusiastically. Cullen lifted his hand and waved it around the garden. There was a brilliant flash of light.

Chapter 40

Later that evening. Brandy's friends sat around the poker table in the game room playing a not-so-friendly card game. As they laughed and joked around over their drinks, Cullen sat at the bar with Nadia, Raven, and Brandy. Brandy flicked her finger at her whiskey glass, trying to move it, but became frustrated when it didn't budge. She sat rigid in her chair and groaned.

"I don't get it," Brandy scoffed. "I was ripping doors off their hinges, throwing flaming balls, and making statues come to life a few hours ago. Now, I can't even move a glass." She suspiciously eyed Cullen. "Did that comfort spell somehow kill my powers?"

Cullen chuckled softly and shook his head. "You didn't lose anything, and I couldn't take them away from you even if I wanted to," he informed her.

"You were pushed to the limits in a fight or flight situation," Raven remarked while his smile almost mocked her. "Your survival instincts kicked in, and you were able to tap into the power already inside you.

Things you've used in the past, possibly without even knowing it."

"Like the whole panther thing?" Brandy asked.

"Exactly," Raven replied. "But now that you're more relaxed, it crept back into your subconscious. Lying dormant."

"Now, the real work starts," Cullen informed her. "You'll need to *learn* how to use your powers. How to control them."

Brandy's expression dropped. "You mean, I'll have to go to some fancy school in London?" she gasped, horrified at the thought.

"No, nothing like that," Cullen replied. "You just need a little guidance from someone with experience." He offered a tiny, playful smile. "A father, perhaps."

"Or a friend of the family," Raven announced and winked at her.

Brandy hid her smile, although her slightly flushed cheeks gave her away. Cullen glared at Raven, somehow displeased by the suggestion.

"Did I miss something?" Cullen asked somewhat gruffly.

"No," Raven replied casually while sipping his whiskey. "I mean, I kept her company while she showered once, but that was nothing."

Cullen continued glaring at Raven's profile. "Excuse me?" he snarled.

Raven looked at Cullen and grinned. "You gave me permission to ask her out, remember?"

"And I already regret it," Cullen scoffed.

"He's just messing with you," Brandy announced, then playfully swatted Raven's arm. "Behave."

Raven chuckled but didn't clarify his earlier shower comment. Cullen frowned and shook his head before taking a swallow of his scotch.

"He's been a pain in my ass for nearly six decades," Cullen remarked. "How we ever became friends, I'll never know."

"You weren't a model warlock in your younger days either," Raven reminded him. "I have some stories--"

"I'd love to hear those," Nadia eagerly chirped, now interested.

"You only think you want to hear those stories," Cullen informed her. "But you're not ready to hear tales from a warlock's youth. I don't want to have to earn your respect all over again."

Nadia clung to Cullen's arm, lovingly stared into his eyes, and smiled. "You're right," she announced. "Perhaps another time. You were gone for weeks, and then I thought you were dead. I have big plans for you."

Cullen eyed her and grinned. "Hmm, I like the way that sounds."

"Too bad nothing exciting ever happens anymore," Randall announced from the poker table. "Life has just become too boring."

Cullen knowingly chuckled softly to himself. Brandy wished she could tell Randall what had happened to him that he *didn't* know about.

"I'll take boring," Nadia muttered while sipping her drink.

"I'll drink to that," Brandy announced and clinked glasses with her mother.

"Hey, Cullen," Randall called to the man at the bar. "About those antiques in your basement--"

Cullen immediately glanced at his watch. "Look at the time," he announced, now in a hurry to escape. "Gotta fly." He pulled Nadia into his arms, then turned to Brandy and smiled cheerfully. "I'm taking your mother for dinner in Paris." Cullen then looked back at Randall and grinned. "Nothing in the basement is real, just great replicas."

Cullen turned to Brandy, kissed her cheek, and then smiled at Raven before leaving the room with Nadia.

Randall appeared bewildered and shook his head. "Somehow, I don't believe he's telling the truth," he remarked.

"Give it a rest, Randall," Clair announced with a low groan. "Seriously, where do you think he'd be able to get authentic, medieval antiques in this day and age?"

Brandy hid her smile and looked at Raven. He returned the smile and took her hand, kissing the back of it. Eva finally folded her cards and left the table, approaching Raven and Brandy.

"Amazing little spell your father used," Eva remarked. "That story about your father surviving the boat accident really seems to have worked. I especially loved how he made everyone forget about Gilford. That was pure warlock gold."

"It's better than the reality of what really happened this weekend," Raven insisted.

"Oh, I wouldn't say it was a total wash-up," Eva remarked. "Considering none of us were seriously hurt, it was actually rather exciting." She then reconsidered her comment. "Except for poor Jana, but she kind of got what she deserved." Eva eyed Raven, then Brandy. "And you don't exactly appear to be suffering either."

"What about you?" Brandy asked. "You had feelings for Ford, well, Dexter. Admit it. You may have felt better not remembering that part."

"I need to remember my mistakes so that I can learn from them," Eva reminded her. "I had a good time with Dexter while it lasted." She then hesitated and frowned. "Then he tried to kill my friends, put me in a dress, was eaten by a mermaid, and turned to stone." Eva shrugged, attempting to hide her grin. "Always a proper ending to a less-than-perfect relationship. Besides, I'm anticipating the possibility of meeting a nice warlock myself."

"At least you've got a sense of humor about the whole ordeal," Raven remarked.

"Not a sense of humor, an incurable curiosity, and a master plan," Eva announced. "I'll see you two in the morning."

Eva flashed Cullen's phone book, smiled daringly, and left the room.

Raven shook his head and laughed while standing. "I hope she stays away from the ones under seventy," Raven remarked, then looked at Brandy with a pleasant smile while pulling her to her feet and into his arms. "What about you? Would you consider dating an older man?"

Brandy appeared to sink into thought, then smiled slyly. "Now that depends," she replied. "Perhaps if he were a warlock. I've recently developed a thing for warlocks."

Raven held her in his arms and moaned softly. "I know just the guy," he announced. "Although he can be a bit of a wolf at times, I think you'll like him."

Brandy laughed softly, then kissed him warmly on the lips. He pulled away, growled playfully, and then kissed her passionately.

§

In the garden, the outdoor lights cast a warm, romantic glow along the pathway. Water cascaded from the upper tier of the water fountain and ran down into the wading pool at the bottom. The stone mermaid remained affixed to the side of the fountain, looking almost natural. A small crack suddenly appeared.

The End

Other books by Holly Copella!
Reviews left on Amazon are appreciated!

"The Battle for Andrea Maria"

A cruise ship attack turns six survivors into overnight celebrities after they take credit for the heroic act of a stowaway who died saving them.

The cruise is just what Jess needed--a bit of harmless fun far from her daily grind. But what begins as a relaxing vacation turns into a desperate fight for her life when terrorists take over the ship and start piling up bodies. Teaming up with a mysterious stowaway, Jess attempts to send out a distress call but knows they cannot wait for help to come. If she or the few remaining passengers have any hope for survival, Jess must act now. The papers dub it "The Battle for *Andrea Maria*," but to Jess it is the moment she fought side-by-side with her enigmatic Romeo, saving the ship--and losing him. She thinks the story ends there, but really, the nightmare is just beginning...

"Insanely Deadly"

When the dead return to life, it's up to an admiral's daughter and a mildly insane, former war hero to save their small town.

Jetta Cross, a Navy Admiral's daughter, is tasked with keeping her father's comrade, a former war hero turned town crazy, grounded in the real world. Capt. John Hunter is still fighting the war in his head, where imaginary dead people are part of his world. When a viral outbreak brings about a zombie uprising, Hunter is left to his own devices. He must resume his role as a one-man commando unit in order to destroy the ravenous undead. With Hunter still fighting his own inner demons as well as the undead, the townspeople fear their zombie neighbors may not be the only threat. Stranded at the island's luxurious resort with a handful of workers, Jetta is forced to live up to her father's reputation and take charge of the deteriorating situation at the hotel. She must wage her own war against the infected before the government declares her hometown a total loss.

"Deadly Institution"

A town recluse suspected of killing his wife teams up with a young woman in order to stop a killer.

After being accused of murdering his wife, Konrad Churchill turns his back on the town that once adored him. Ten years later, he still holds his grudge and the title of the most feared man in town. With the reopening of the burned mental institution, where his wife had died, former employees are now murdered one by one, throwing suspicion back on Churchill. A young local reporter, Jacey, is forced to reveal her long-time friendship with the infamous recluse in order to clear his name not only in the recent murders but to exonerate him in the death of his wife as well. Will Jacey's relationship with Churchill invite the killer closer to her? Or is the killer already in her life?

"Death Displacement"

A grief-stricken man travels back in time to seek revenge on the woman who murdered his girlfriend, but inadvertently falls in love with her.

Kane is about to marry the woman he loves. His life is perfect. A few weeks before the wedding, a vindictive woman from his girlfriend's past mysteriously arrives and kills her. He learns of a traumatic accident that happened five years earlier, which triggers Riley's hatred for his girlfriend. Distraught over his girlfriend's death, Kane uses an antique time machine to travel into the past in order to find and destroy the woman responsible. When he runs into Riley's younger self, he realizes she's not the monster she later becomes, and he can't bring himself to destroy her. With a little help from his oddball friend from the past, they formulate a plan to prevent the accident that sends Riley down her destructive path. Kane's plan backfires when he falls for the younger Riley. His new tortured existence is further complicated when future Riley, his girlfriend's killer, shows up with her own devious agenda that doesn't include him. Will he be able to stop the time ripple, which ultimately ends with his girlfriend's death? Or will future Riley take him out of the timeline forever--

"Dead Village"

After strange happenings isolate a small resort town from the rest of the world, nearly one hundred residents seek refuge at the closed hotel. Only eight survive the night. And that's just the beginning...

One day after the entire population of Fox Ridge Village disappears, a car wreck forces several unsuspecting crash victims to seek help at the closed summer hotel. Within the hotel, they discover the grisly aftermath of a brutal slaughter. Crash victims Vander and Devon, a reluctant clairvoyant, team up to solve the riddle of the "haunted hotel" and the mass hysteria plaguing the remaining survivors. By the time they discover the hotel's secret, they're already drawn into the hysteria. As the body count continues to climb, it's a race to isolate the source and bring everyone back to reality before they kill one another. Will Devon be able to communicate with the traumatized spirits before their fate becomes her own?

"Town Darling"

After surviving a brutal attack that claims the lives of those she loves, a young woman seeks revenge on a corrupt town.

Going back home is never easy, but for Casey, it means returning to her corrupt hometown, where she barely survived a brutal attack. Accompanied by two family friends, she seeks justice for the night that destroyed her life. Her physical scars are nothing compared to her emotional ones, forcing the local sheriff to believe that the town darling is back for revenge. As the conspiracy for her revenge appears to be leading up to the coveted town fair, the sheriff is determined to stop her from fulfilling her vengeful scheme...but guilt over his role on that fateful night continues to haunt him. Will his desperate need for Casey's forgiveness be his undoing? Or will Casey's desire for revenge destroy them both?

"Basement Dwellers"

A viral outbreak at a hospital leaves a mortician, sheriff, and coroner fighting for their lives against a horde of undead and the CDC.

After a massive car wreck leaves several survivors in critical condition at the local hospital, a surgeon uses experimental drugs on his critical patients and accidentally causes a zombie outbreak. When local mortician, Lexx, receives an infected corpse as her client, she becomes stranded in the hospital basement during CDC quarantine along with the local sheriff and the coroner. The infamous surgeon struggles to find a cure for his infectious blunder by using the other survivors as test subjects. Meanwhile, Lexx and the sheriff attempt to locate his missing sister, who's stranded somewhere in the battle zone that once was the emergency room. It's a race against time and the ravenous undead. Can they survive the undead before the CDC sanitizes the hospital of all infection?

"Misfits, Inc."

A seemingly ordinary young woman meets four misfits who claim she has given them supernatural powers.

While on a business trip to a remote island paradise, a bored secretary, Hailey, has her world turned upside down when her path collides with a psychic freak, Skyler. He attempts to convince her that they had met in his dreams, and she had chosen him as one of her four mystic warriors. After Skyler foresees a woman's death, they discover an unidentified creature has killed one of the guests. They are joined by a lounge pianist and a rich playboy, who also claim they had met her in their dreams. If Skyler's prophecies are genuine, the evil entity controlling the ravenous creatures needs to destroy Hailey to ensure its survival. Reluctantly accepting her fate, Hailey has to locate the last and most powerful of her chosen warriors, The Guardian. Their fate is in doubt when The Guardian turns out to be a self-absorbed, former cat burglar with a bad attitude. Can Hailey turn her company of misfits into an elite team of mystic warriors? Or will The Guardian's secret agenda destroy them all?

"Deadly Institution 2"

When blackmail turns into murder, a young woman finds herself caught in the killer's crosshairs.

The small town of Stony Ridge is no stranger to scandal and persecution of the innocent. When a brutal killing shakes the town's prestigious country club, Jacey McMurray seeks help from a self-proclaimed vigilante, Konrad Churchill. As her professional and personal worlds collide, Jacey fears the stress of the country club killings have finally taken their toll on Churchill. Can a stressed-out vigilante stop the killer before he strikes again?

"Witness Protection"
Also available in audiobook!

After witnessing an execution, a resourceful young woman attempts to disappear while being pursued by a hitman and a handsome federal agent.

A helicopter pilot, Jackie Remus, reluctantly agrees to go on a date with one of her clients, but her date is unexpectedly cut short when she witnesses a man being murdered. After narrowly escaping with her life, she is placed into protective custody. When the safe house is breached, Jackie makes a daring escape from both the hired killers and the handsome FBI agent, who wants to return her to protective custody. With a little help from her sly and crafty friend, Monroe, Jackie is convinced she can disappear until the trial. While on her journey to meet with her friend, she solicits help from a few shady but lovable characters along the way. Although she manages to stay one step ahead of the hired killers, the federal agent remains in hot pursuit. Will Jackie reach Monroe before she's captured by the FBI and returned to protective custody? Or will the hired killers silence her first?

"Unconditional"

A young woman puts her life on hold to care for an unstable, highly skilled combat soldier, who believes someone is trying to kill him.

A botched military coup leaves a team of elite fighters injured, with one clinging to life in a coma. When Harlan wakes from his coma, he's left with no memory of his past life. His commander's daughter, Indy, takes it upon herself to care for the fallen war hero. She's challenged with more than just his physical care as she combats with not only his memory loss but also his newly found desire for her. His infatuation with her becomes the least of her worries when he sinks back into his role of a combat soldier. Believing his life is in danger, his fighting skills emerge, transforming him into an unpredictable and dangerous man. Will his memory return to him before Indy is forced to commit him? Or will he finally find his nemesis, "the coyote", and possibly claim the life of an innocent person?

"The Pen Pal"

In order to save her friend, she must enter the mind of a serial killer.

When her best friend is abducted, no one believes Jolynn saw it in a psychic vision. With nowhere to turn, Jolynn reluctantly joins Agent Harris Slade and his team on their hunt for a sadistic serial killer known only as "The Pen Pal". Finally confronted with the killer, Jolynn realizes she must enter the mind of the psychopath in order to stop the brutal killings. But when her vision reveals a particularly disturbing death, can Jolynn sacrifice her lover for her friend?

"Witness Protection 2"
The Return of Whiskey Tango Foxtrot

Believing she holds the clue to millions in missing laundered money, a young woman is placed into the protective care of a former Navy SEAL team.

Feeling sorry for her recently separated co-worker, Leeann invites Wiley to join her and her friends on their night out. Little does she know that finding her co-worker murdered is just the beginning of her nightmare. Leeann unknowingly holds the key to fifty million dollars in potentially laundered mob money. With hired killers pursuing her, the FBI places her into a different kind of protective custody. Former Navy SEAL team Whiskey Tango Foxtrot reunites to keep Leeann alive at their secret hideaway. What should be an easy assignment takes an unscheduled turn when secrets, lies, and betrayal threaten to derail their mission. Is the team prepared for a war on their own doorstep? Will Leeann's misguided trust endanger the lives of those sent to protect her?

"Witness Protection 3"
Alpha Mike Foxtrot

A helicopter pilot risks her life to help a team of retired Navy SEALs rescue two girls from a killer.

When former Navy SEAL team Whiskey Tango Foxtrot asks for a simple favor, Jackie reluctantly offers her air-taxi services. What could go wrong? What begins as a search and rescue for two girls turns into a fight for survival against a heavily armed drug cartel. Wanted by the law with the cartel in hot pursuit and their home base breached, the team is forced to call in a favor from a questionable ally. Unfortunately, their new safe house isn't what it seems. Without knowing who the real enemy is, can Jackie and the team save their young witnesses from the hands of a killer?

"Already Dead"
Supernatural Collection

From the already dead to the undead. Three supernatural tales of "things that go bump in the night".

"Bloodletting" - A vampire-themed resort allows guests to *participate* in their Bloodletting Ritual to celebrate the island's legendary vampires.

"Reaper of Souls" - A young woman must outwit an evil sorcerer in order to save her brother or become one of his minions forever.

"Already Dead" - When Flight 220 crashes, ten passengers make it to an isolated island, but only one man lives to tell the lie.

"Witness Protection 4"
O-Dark-Hundred

A simple assignment turns deadly when a retired Navy SEAL team uncovers a plot to kill a notorious mob boss.

When Whiskey Tango Foxtrot embarks on a simple stalking case, they're not prepared for a trip to a private island paradise owned by an infamous mobster. With one of their own suffering from traumatic head injuries, the team is left scrambling to decide what is real or imagined. The situation escalates even further when they uncover an assassination plot where everyone is a suspect. Now targets themselves, can the team survive their trip to paradise?

"Witness Protection 5"
Outside the Wire

After suffering several casualties on their last assignment, a retired Navy SEAL team discovers their misery is just beginning.

When Whiskey Tango Foxtrot returns home after suffering a devastating loss, they're hit with even more bad news regarding the rest of their team. Their grief is cut short when they discover their names are all on the same hit list. Hunted by relentless assassins, the scattered team must decide whether to remain safely hidden or find the man who put the price on their heads. Against the wishes of her teammates, Jackie strikes out on her own in order to save a friend who wants her dead. In a kill-or-be-killed situation, will Jackie's emotions finally betray her?

"The Murder of Emily Fisher"

After finding their favorite teacher murdered, the lives of two teenage girls are forever changed.

Everyone loved Emily Fisher. While walking home one afternoon, two teenage girls, Sidney and Trisha, stumble upon a gruesome murder scene. The brutal murder of Emily Fisher, a young, attractive schoolteacher, shocks the small town of **Marilina**. After graduation, Sidney moves far away from the memories of the small town, while Trisha retreats deeper into denial. Eight years after the murder, Sidney receives a desperate call from her childhood friend, forcing her to return home. Trisha believes Emily's killer was falsely accused, and she manages to turn the entire town against her while attempting to prove it. When Trisha receives a death threat, Sidney realizes there may be some credibility to her friend's wild accusations. Is Trisha's mental breakdown a result of childhood trauma? Or is the real killer actually attempting to silence her? In order to save her friend, Sidney must answer the eight-year-old question. Who murdered Emily Fisher?

"Once Upon a Disaster"

A young homicide detective finds herself at the mercy of a hitman in the aftermath of an earthquake.

While investigating the murder of a hitman, Detective Jade Wesson pursues a lead connecting the dead man to a break-in at a computer programming company. She's drawn into the world of a nightclub owner and front man for the mob, Cody Riley. Her investigation continues to point to Cody's right-hand man and possible hitman, Vahn Lott. Despite her efforts to keep her investigation on track, Vahn has plans of his own for the attractive detective. When an unprecedented earthquake rocks their east coast town, Jade must put her life in Vahn's hands if she wants to survive. Can she trust a man who might be the killer she's hunting?

"Awaken the Dead"

A grieving innkeeper struggles to keep her haunted hotel out of foreclosure.

After losing her parents in a suspicious boating accident, Harley Brandon is determined to keep the family hotel out of foreclosure. Unfortunately, the hotel ghosts have other plans. Built with tainted money, the century-old Horizon Hotel thrives on a tradition of murder, scandal, and suicide. As the paranormal activity increases to alarming levels, Harley discovers the truth about the hotel and its residents. Can Harley save her friends from the hotel's frightening hidden secrets?

"Castle Bloodshed"
Murder Collection

From a deadly island paradise to haunted castles. Three novella-length tales of murder, mystery, and malicious intent.

"Castle Bloodshed" – A tour of Wesley Castle turns into a fight for survival as six stranded tourists discover the haunting secrets within the castle walls. A mystery writer teams up with an uptight butler in order to stop a killer who may already be dead. Novella-length paranormal murder mystery.

"Fleshies" – Is Uncle Rutger crazy? Five years ago, four business partners died within their newly purchased, fixer-upper castle. Their bodies were never found. The surviving partner, Rutger, claims a demon keeps him as its slave. Rutger's nephew schemes to save his uncle by sacrificing the lives of a group of stranded motorists and a high-profile novelist. Novella-length supernatural murder mystery.

"Demon Island" – A group of strangers are invited to a remote island for the reading of a will. The guests soon discover they were brought to the island to be executed one by one. It's up to a private detective and a tenacious young woman to solve the murders and find a way to escape paradise. Novella-length murder mystery.

"Brighton Island"

When a psychic visits a haunted island mansion, he inadvertently awakens the ghosts' tortured souls.

Something's not right with Simon. When Jacklyn brings her eccentric friend to her uncle's island mansion, she doesn't expect him to slip into psychic overload. As Simon attempts to solve a decade-old double homicide, Jacklyn is confronted with the possibility that she could be next to join the mansion ghosts. When they find themselves stranded on the secluded island, her Uncle Hyland wages his own war to save them from a flesh-and-blood killer. Will her uncle's "shock and awe" military tactics save them or get them killed? Can Simon bring peace to the tortured souls or unexpectedly join them?

"A.L.F. Resort"

A fantasy vacation turns into a nightmare when the resort's artificial life forms are compromised.

Welcome to A.L.F. Resort, where you can live out your fantasies with safe, state-of-the-art artificial life form robots! When a young journalist and a photographer are sent to A.L.F. Resort to do a story for their magazine, Shay and Becka believe they've hit the jackpot of all work-cations. The engineers pull out all the stops to make their fantasies a memorable experience. Unfortunately, the newly designed A.L.F., the Gen X, is smarter than his programming and creates havoc within Shay's fantasy. A computer malfunction removes their safety inhibitors, and the A.L.F.s play out their own hostile fantasies. Zombies, bikers, and mobsters run amok, turning fantasies into nightmares. Shay gets more of a story than she anticipates, but will she survive long enough to write it?

"Jungle Princess"

While stranded on a prison island, a young woman discovers a creature of "unknown" origin.

After their cruise ship sinks, Alex and two of her shipmates are stranded on a deserted, tropical island. Unfortunately, the castaways soon realize they're not alone. They discover an abandoned prison with over two dozen inmates living on the island's south side. While avoiding the prison on the far side of the island, Alex discovers a strange but loveable creature of unknown origin. When one of her fellow castaways is in trouble, Alex reluctantly seeks help from the prisoners. After the brutal murder of several inmates, their questions surrounding the abandoned prison are about to be answered. What really killed over one hundred prisoners? And is it still out there?

"Murder in Wax"

A series of brutal murders plagues a quiet farming community when beautiful women audition for the same acting job.

While all the young women in town are fighting over a once-in-a-lifetime acting opportunity, Devon Vincent is excited about her new job at the local wax museum. Although supportive of her friend's acting aspirations, Devon has a hard time understanding the rivalry among the women in town. When the aspiring actresses are brutally murdered one by one, Devon fears her friend may be the next victim. Devon finds herself in the middle of a murderous revenge plot that leads back to the wax museum's doorstep and possibly implicates her boss as the killer. Will Devon's newly found feelings for her boss bring a killer closer to her? Or is the killer already in her circle?

"Witness Protection 6"
Alpha Dogs

An easy rescue turns into a wild ride for retired Navy SEAL team Whiskey Tango Foxtrot when everyone wants to kill their client.

It was a simple task. Rescue a young woman from her mob boss father-in-law. Little did Jackie and company realize that rescuing the young woman was the easy part. Keeping her alive would be a massive undertaking, especially when everyone wants a piece of the mafia heiress. The team fights for survival against their toughest adversaries yet. How many innocent people must die in order to save one woman? Can the team survive the ultimate battle between mercenaries and assassins?

"Midnight Requisition"

A series of brutal murders leaves a traumatized young woman on a hunt to find a killer.

When they were just babies, Scorpio and her twin brother, Kane, tragically lost their parents under mysterious circumstances. Refusing to accept his father was dead, Kane set off on a mission to find a man he'd never met. A home invasion gone wrong leaves Scorpio grieving the loss of those she loves. Out of the tragedy of her loss, two fallen heroes are thrust upon her. Scorpio soon realizes someone wants her dead, and the killer may already be in her circle. As her entire life unravels in a web of betrayal and lies, can Scorpio trust her new, slightly questionable friends?

"Until Death"

Liars, cheaters, blackmail, and murder. It would be a wedding no one would forget.

Despite knowing he's making the biggest mistake of his life, Raina Steele reluctantly attends her father's third wedding. What should have been a boring reception turns into a web of lies, betrayal, and murder. With no one above suspicion, Raina must put aside her feud with the arrogant yet insanely handsome butler in order to catch the killer before he finds his next victim. With a murderer waiting to strike and lives hanging in the balance, the real question remains...the bride is wearing white? Seriously?

"Tainted"

What happens at the Dark Forest Hotel, stays at the Dark Forest Hotel...for all eternity.

What secrets surround Dark Forest Hotel? After her parents die under mysterious circumstances, sixteen-year-old Jeri escapes foster care and seeks refuge at a "closed for the season" hotel. Over the next six years, Jeri graduates from teenage runaway to the hotel's assistant general manager. When she learns a convention is secretly held every year in her absence, she demands answers from her boss, friends, and co-workers. After getting conflicting stories, Jeri sets out to discover the truth. She's suddenly thrown into a horrifying new world where vampires and vicious creatures are craving her virgin blood. After six years of being lied to, is there anyone she can trust?

"Witness Protection 7"
Bravo Foxtrot

An Army deserter on the run brings mayhem to a retired Navy SEAL team when his teenage daughter is caught in a mercenary's cross-hairs.

A weekend of fun turns into a race for survival as Monique and Colleen's surrogate big brother, Bogart, rescues the girls from mercenaries hunting Colleen's Army deserter father. With the girls safely stashed at their Colorado hideaway, trouble brews when the team discovers Colleen's father was framed by his former commander over a stolen, high-tech weapon. In order to clear Colleen's father and bring him home, the team must fight one of their toughest adversaries yet...a high-ranking military officer with countless mercenaries and the U.S. military behind him.

"Midnight Requisition 2"
Amateur Night

A brother and sister duo team up to catch a potential kidnapper.

After finally reuniting with her not-so-dead brother, Scorpio and her friends are taunted into helping him with his new case. A wealthy cattle rancher believes someone wants to abduct his daughter, but the team suspects her ex-boyfriend is pulling off an elaborate scheme to win her back. What appears to be a slice of paradise in the Colorado Mountains turns out to be a venomous snake pit filled with lies, lust, betrayal, and murder. Surviving the depraved family becomes the least of the team's worries when a botched kidnapping turns into murder.

"Cemetery Stalkers" Horror Collection

Four tales of horror from flesh-eating alien monsters to blood-sucking vampires.

"Night Creatures" – When a rescue party becomes stranded on an abandoned cruise ship, they discover the terrifying secret unleashed from the cargo hold. What starts out as a rescue mission rapidly deteriorates into survival as a frightening creature with a taste for human flesh hunts the small group. Novella-length horror book.

"Ravenous" – After escaping a carjacking in the back woods, a young woman seeks refuge in a mysterious mansion with a terrifying secret. Despite promises of a ride to town in the morning, she's convinced she's being held prisoner by a cult leader. Short paranormal story.

"The Feast" – Five years ago, a killer went on a murderous rampage at the church picnic. Despite eyewitness accounts of a non-human killer, the local law refused to believe the town's citizens. When a group of teenagers stumble upon the contained remains of the killer, they unwittingly set him free to continue his terror upon the small town. Novella-length paranormal book.

"Cemetery Stalkers" – When 'The Reaper' stalks a cemetery, death follows. Following a series of bizarre incidents within the cemetery, a young woman fears for the safety of her friend, who lives in the middle of spook central. Short horror story.

"Jumpers"

When a cruise ship is exposed to a deadly virus, the fate of the world rests in the hands of a lounge dancer and a conman.

An infectious outbreak threatens the passengers and crew of the "Queen Anita" and the entire world if the virus escapes back into civilization. Lounge dancer, Maxine, must find a way to prevent the destruction of the world, but in order to do that, she needs to trust a conman with unique insight into the virus.

"Witness Protection 8"
Midnight Requisition

A brother and sister duo find themselves on an explosive collision course with a team of retired Navy SEALs.

Obsessed with the belief that his father is still alive, Kane Wayland embarks on a foolhardy mission to confront the elusive former Navy SEAL, Zack Kinsley. Despite heavy protests, Kane's sister, Scorpio, joins him on his quest. The disastrous "reunion" comes with a steep price that none are prepared to pay. With the haunting reality of the botched mission, Midnight Requisition, still looming over each of them, can the two teams pull together in time to prevent another tragedy?

"Midnight Requisition 3"
Circular Run

A brother and sister reopen a hotel with a tainted history, only to discover its past refuses to stay dead and buried.

Scorpio and Kane Wayland finally realize their dream of reopening their grandfather's old, cliffside hotel in Maine. With the hotel's checkered past behind it, the relaunch is a dream come true. Unfortunately, history has a tendency to repeat itself. When guests mysteriously vanish, the hotel's somewhat seedy clientele are all now suspects. In order to save their hotel, Scorpio and Kane must stop a killer. When your guests are mercenaries, bounty hunters, and mobsters, who can you trust?

"Raven Force"

An innkeeper becomes involved in a game of espionage after picking up a mysterious hitchhiker.

After surviving a nightmare of a date, Maxine Croft didn't think her evening could get any worse...until she nearly hits a stranger on a dark back road. This unprecedented meeting would turn Max's world upside down as she's thrust into a world of murder, corruption, and deception within her own backyard. As she gets in deeper with an elite, special task force, Max inadvertently puts her sisters' lives in danger. Will Max and her sisters become just more "collateral damage" to facilitate the team's mission?

"Midnight Requisition 4"
Charlie Foxtrot

A mob convention at a remote cliffside hotel has murderous consequences.

Hotel owner, Scorpio Wayland, reluctantly books a "mob" convention at her quiet, cliffside resort. What could go wrong? When former mob boss Salvatore Romano invites friends for a "family" reunion, disaster swiftly follows.

"Witness Protection 9"
S.N.A.F.U.

A notorious mob boss turns to a retired Navy SEAL team to keep his son alive.

They were made an offer they couldn't refuse. When his son is accused of murdering known mobsters throughout Colorado, Giovanni turns to the retired Navy SEAL team of Whiskey Tango Foxtrot to keep his boy alive and prevent a war between the "families". With the mobster's son in the crosshairs of every hitman and bounty hunter on the West Coast, Jackie and the boys need to find Marco and go completely off-grid. But is the team risking their lives to protect a serial killer?

"Witness Protection 10"
Bravo Zulu

It's all hands on deck when the mob declares war on the team and those they love.

Whiskey Tango Foxtrot reunites with Midnight Requisition when war is declared by a notorious mobster and his army of highly trained soldiers. After several deadly attacks shake both teams, their skills, loyalties, and limitations are tested in an explosive and bloody rampage that will scar and change their lives forever.

"Pretty Little Dead Things"

Romance, scandal, and an unsolved murder. Welcome to snob central!

After a disastrous evening at the exclusive country club gala, Marley Temple doesn't think her life can get any worse. When someone close to her is murdered, Marley is left devastated. Although everyone else seems to move on after the unsolved homicide, Marley can't let it go. She's suddenly thrust into the inner circle of a wealthy playwright recluse, whose stage actress wife was brutally butchered just two years earlier. Although Marley fears falling for the infamous Devlin Ryker, forming a strange alliance with him brings her closer to solving the perplexing murder. But as she gets closer to learning the truth, the killer gets closer to her. Will Marley discover the killer's identity before she becomes his next victim?

"Dead Again"

After barely surviving a murderous attack, a young woman believes a cold-hearted cattle rancher holds clues to that night.

After the murder of her mother in an attack that nearly claimed her life as well, Sage Remington believes moving to the country with her sister will heal her emotional scars. Sage's near-death experience leaves her with memory loss surrounding that fateful night. A bizarre encounter with an infamous cattle rancher, Jackson Morgan, brings back fragments of Sage's lost memory. If she wants to piece together what happened to her mother, Sage needs to get closer to Jackson, who somehow holds the clues. Unfortunately, discovering Jackson's secrets opens the door to a whole other world where nothing is what it seems.

"Dead Woods"

Two magazine reporters get more of a story than they want while investigating strange happenings in a cursed forest.

While interviewing a small-town hero, two adventure-seeking magazine reporters, Kara and Lenox, hike into the infamous Dead Woods in search of a story. Their simple outing takes a chilling turn, and they soon find themselves involved in the town's haunted history filled with curses, witch burnings, and zombified minions. Narrowly escaping with her life, Kara runs into local legend Daemon Archer, a distant relative of a man accused of witchcraft and burned in Town Square in the 1800s. In order to survive a panic-stricken village prophesizing 'evil will take a mate', Kara has to trust the town's most feared citizen.

"Cinderella of Yardley Manor"

Never believing in love at first sight, a young woman finally thinks she's met the man of her dreams, only to discover he's the wrong man.

After graduating college, Ramsey O'Connell reluctantly agrees to travel with her uncle on his business trip to England. However, when she discovers her uncle's true intention--to fix her up with his wealthy colleague, William Yardley —she has some reservations. Falling in love was the last thing she expected, but falling in love with an emotionally unavailable man turns her fairytale into a nightmare.

"Protect and Serve"

Celebrating her birthday with friends on a luxury cruise ship, a young heiress is looking for a little romance on the high seas. Instead, she's confronted by kidnappers and assassins.

Kasey's birthday celebration cruise was supposed to be ten days of sun, sea, and fun with her friends. That is, until her uncle insists she take her bodyguard along. Although her bodyguard, Hunter, is undeniably handsome, he's a little rough around the edges. When her uncle's enemies exact their revenge on Kasey, the cruise turns into a nightmare. If they want to survive, they have to trust Hunter. But sometimes, the enemy is not who you think.

"Crime Scene"

The cast of a popular television crime show finds themselves stranded in a small town after a real-life murder mystery intrudes on their world of make-believe.

After weeks of filming on location, the cast of a highly acclaimed crime show becomes stranded when their luxury bus breaks down in the middle of nowhere. An inconvenient overnight in a small town turns into the beginning of a murder investigation with the cast of "Crime Scene" high on the suspect list. To save the cast's reputation, the show's writer assists the handsome but guarded sheriff and his K-9 deputy in the murder investigation. As alibis unravel, lies pile up, and the suspect list grows, can they catch the killer before he strikes again?

"Midnight Requisition 5"
Sierra Hotel

A Christmas wedding, mistletoe, and murder.

Only a few days before Christmas, a very pregnant Scorpio and her friends are planning Mac and Maverick's wedding. Little did they know that Santa would be delivering a few early presents. What was supposed to be a merry Christmas turns into an epic whodunit when a helicopter crashes on the hotel grounds, leaving eight stranded passengers and a dead man. Their once silent night is filled with accusations, alibis, and mayhem. With the assistance of former Special Agent Holden Falcone, can they solve the murders before the next body drops?

"The Rancher's Daughter"

When her town, ranch, and life are threatened, a young woman teams up with the enemy's top enforcer to reclaim what is hers.

Skyler Winchester's small hometown has become more corrupt in the five years since her parents' car accident. Little by little, wealthy business tycoon Marcus has been buying buildings, property, and people. As one of the largest ranch owners and the object of Marcus's lust, Sky has always been immune to the corruption and dirty dealings, but her friends aren't so lucky. After forming an unholy alliance with one of Marcus's top enforcers, it appears that Sky's immunity has been revoked. When her life is threatened, will the man she trusts most be the one sent to eliminate her?

"Beyond the Fence Line"

In the dust of a modern cattle ranch, a girl with wrangler dreams and her childhood protector build a bond that falters under unvoiced desires.

On a sprawling modern cattle ranch, two kids bound by loss forge an unbreakable bond. After losing his mother when he was only ten years old, Brandt wants nothing to do with the fatherless five-year-old ragamuffin, Mazie, whose mother runs the ranch house. But as years of dust and dreams shape them, he becomes her protector, and she his constant shadow, chasing her goal to wrangle cattle alongside him. Their friendship is unshakable until one reckless night sparks a truth Brandt has always known: he loves her. Mazie can't see past their childhood bond, and the rift tears them apart. Several years later, with the ranch as the only home they've known, they must confront their past, their pain, and the love that's waited years to claim its truth. A story of resilience, loyalty, and a romance forged in the grit of the open range, spanning years of heartache and hope.

"Nature of the Beast"

She claimed her father's cursed mansion...where the ghosts within the walls have long been waiting for her.

When Brandy Holloway inherits a sprawling country mansion from the father she never knew, she expects secrets, not literal skeletons in the closets. The gothic estate has all the comforts of the "Psycho" house and all the charm of "The Addams Family" home. The young maid swears it's haunted, and the handsome, mysterious butler hides secrets of his own. After Brandy invites her friends for a weekend escape, the fun turns deadly when, one by one, they vanish into the house's endless depths. Trapped in a ghostly home that hungers for souls, Brandy must team up with her eccentric butler to uncover the mansion's bloodstained secrets before she becomes its prisoner...forever.

Coming Soon!

"Past Lies"

&

"Witness Protection 11"

ABOUT THE AUTHOR

Holly Copella has been writing since the age of twelve when her frustration at a book's poor plot drove her to author her own story. Over the last decade, she's written a number of screenplays, some of which she's now adapting into novels. Her fascination with zombies and other darker material lends an edge to her writing, which tends to lean toward horror. As a fan of Agatha Christie, she appreciates the craft of a good plot and the importance of creating significant characters.

Hailing from Pennsylvania, Copella lives in the Endless Mountains on a farm with her horse, Maverick, new puppy, Darth, and other animals. In addition to writing and reading fiction, she enjoys riding horses and traveling to Las Vegas